He wanted Jill. Badly

The thought of being cast in the role of her fiancé, with all those unconscious touches and secret smiles between lovers held a *lot* of appeal.

"Morgan?" Jill touched his arm.

He frowned. "Yeah?"

"Mind if I take off my shoes?" she asked. "It's been a long day."

Nodding, his smile was strained as she slipped off her navy pumps, her toes curling into the plush carpet. Her toenails were painted, and he was a sucker for that.

He looked closer and almost groaned. *Red. A startling, deep, sensual red.*

He was an even bigger sucker for anything red on a woman. An image of Jill lying before him in a red satin teddy had him nearly losing control.

"I have to kiss you," he murmured. *Rules be damned....*

"You make it sound like a bad thing," she answered breathlessly.

"It is," he replied, reaching for her. "It's *real* bad."

"Bad can be very good, you know," she said in a voice that had his temperature skyrocketing.

Dear Reader,

We're surrounded by rules every single day of our lives. We have rules that tell us to follow the law, rules of the road and rules of conduct. There are even rules on how to clean the coffeemaker!

Jill Cassidy knows all about rules. She's an attorney. Rules are her business. But when she approaches a sexy stranger and asks him to pretend to be her fiancé, she finds herself with a new set to learn—*Rules of Engagement*.

As far as Morgan Price is concerned, the only rule he plans to adhere to is keeping his heart safe from the sweet, sassy lawyer. Little does he know that Jill has every intention of bending that rule to the breaking point.

I enjoyed my time with Jill and Morgan and hope you do as well. And if you're up for a little rule breaking, look for Jill's sister Carly, in my next Temptation—#797 *Breaking the Rules*—out in September 2000.

I love to hear from readers. You can write to me at P.O. Box 224, Mohall, ND 58761 or via e-mail at jamiedenton@weluvromance.com.

Happy reading!

Jamie Denton

Books by Jamie Denton

HARLEQUIN TEMPTATION
708—FLIRTING WITH DANGER
748—THE SEDUCTION OF SYDNEY
767—VALENTINE FANTASY

RULES OF ENGAGEMENT
Jamie Denton

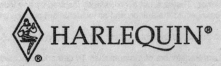

HARLEQUIN®

TORONTO • NEW YORK • LONDON
AMSTERDAM • PARIS • SYDNEY • HAMBURG
STOCKHOLM • ATHENS • TOKYO • MILAN • MADRID
PRAGUE • WARSAW • BUDAPEST • AUCKLAND

You said only I could make my dreams come true.
You said I could do anything.
You said only those who never tried, never succeeded.
As always, Mom, you were right.
This one is for you, with all my love.
Jamie

ISBN 0-373-25893-3

RULES OF ENGAGEMENT

Copyright © 2000 by Jamie Ann Denton.

Visit us at www.eHarlequin.com

Printed in U.S.A.

HE HAD TO BE *the* most gorgeous man on the face of the earth, his well-honed athletic body nothing short of a virtuoso's work of art. Faded jeans hugged strong thighs and a knit polo shirt stretched over a wide chest and lean belly. Raisin-colored sleeves molded and emphasized sculpted, muscular biceps capable of making a girl's heart go all fluttery.

He was also extremely irritated.

Jill Cassidy considered closing the door to her office, but with Mr. Tall, Dark and Gorgeous raising his voice at her boss right outside, the last thing she wanted was to draw attention to herself and perhaps embarrass her boss.

"I do apologize, Morgan," her boss said calmly. "But calendar conflicts make it impossible. I just have no one available to handle such a minor offense."

The Adonis glanced her way. Her breath hitched in her throat, and her mouth suddenly felt drier than the California desert. Hair as black as midnight highlighted eyes the color of thunderclouds, holding her spellbound. High cheekbones and a firm, square jaw added to the sculpted magnificence of his appearance. Even though his features were hardened by his obvious frustration, masculine appeal still radiated from him in waves.

Her feminine senses went on red alert.

Jill's gaze dipped to his mouth, zeroing in on the sensuality of his full lower lip. Forbidden images of touching her lips to his sent a surge of heat racing through her.

Shocked by her reaction to a complete stranger, no matter how gorgeous, she shifted her attention back to the open book on her desk and the case law she needed for a motion to suppress evidence she'd been researching most of the afternoon. Before she looked away, she caught a glimpse of something else in his eyes, something that touched her deep inside. A hint of desperation—an emotion she was far too acquainted with to discount.

"There has to be something you can do," Mr. Wonderful said, his tone calmer. "Someone you can spare."

"It's only a minor offense. Just let the public defender's office handle it if this guy can't afford an attorney," Nick offered. "You can't save them all, Morgan."

Jill shook her head. A public defender was a sure guarantee of a conviction. She knew, since she'd spent six months in the PD's office before landing a job in Lowell and Montgomery's criminal department two years ago. From her experience in the government office, she'd quickly learned that most of the once bright-eyed lawyers were overworked, underpaid and jaded by the revolving-door policy of the criminal justice system.

"He's a good kid, Nick, and I want him to have a *good* lawyer," Morgan insisted. "He doesn't need one mistake haunting him for the rest of his life."

Jill agreed, even if she had no idea who needed an attorney or what crime had been committed. Everyone deserved a good lawyer.

"He's my best foreman," he added, shoving a large hand through his jet-black hair, "and I need him back on the job site as soon as possible. It's important."

Nick shook his head regretfully. "I'm sorry, Morgan," he said. "I wish I could help, but we just don't have anyone to spare. If it was a bigger case, I could see about shifting some things around to make room on the calendar. Look, if the final decision was mine, you know we wouldn't be having this conversation, but I do have other senior partners to answer to."

Jill sensed Morgan's frustration when he shook hands with her boss, then said something she couldn't hear before spinning on his booted heel and heading down the corridor. Which was just as well, she decided. She had her own personal problem for which she still hadn't found a resolution, and panting after a handsome stranger was hardly a way to solve it.

Or was it?

Jill bit her lip as Nick walked into her small, windowless office, his hands shoved in the front pockets of his trousers. "How's the motion coming along?" he asked, stopping in front of her desk.

"Good," she said, her mind whirring with possibilities she couldn't seem to shake. She dropped her pen on the desk, certain she was truly desperate to even consider propositioning a perfect stranger. "What was that all about?"

Nick shook his head again, compassion lighting his distinguished features. "One of his employees tied one on for his twenty-first birthday, got a little out of hand and now he's facing a drunk-and-disorderly charge," he said, dropping into the chair opposite her desk. "I'd like to help, but...well, you heard. Montgomery's been on a rampage lately because he's had more beans in the debt column and less in the income column. If I shifted a bigger case for something small like this, I'd be wearing his wing tips in a very uncomfortable place."

She suppressed a grin and settled back into the hunter-green executive chair. "Can't you take on his case pro bono, and not involve the firm?"

Nick propped his foot over his knee. "I wish I could, but with the Simmons trial in two days and the Martinez trial in another week.... Well, you know what's it been like around here. How many billable hours have you put in the past month on those two cases alone? Montgomery's managing partner for a reason," he said with a heartfelt chuckle.

Jill did understand. Just that morning all of the associates had been called into a meeting with Mr. Montgomery for the semiannual "billable hours are down again" lecture. The firm was in business to make a profit, but the softer side of her, which wasn't completely jaded by the legal system, wanted desperately to reach out to the most stunning man she'd ever laid eyes on and do something to help him.

And it had nothing to do with her physical reaction to Mr. Drop-Dead Gorgeous, she told herself firmly, or the ludicrous idea that had taken hold and wouldn't let go.

Jill quashed the silly notion flirting on the edges of her mind as not only insane, but certifiable. She leaned forward again, bracing her elbows on the desk. "The firm can't take on his case, right?"

Nick shook his head. "Not unless I want to send Montgomery into an apoplectic fit."

The idea wouldn't be nudged, shoved or quashed. "But if you took on his case pro bono, you'd have to assign it to another associate, right?"

Nick's brows pulled together in a frown. "No, Jill," he said firmly, knowing exactly where she was headed with her line of questioning. "Morgan Price is a friend. I want to help him, but there's no way the firm can afford to spare you right now. We've got two tough cases—"

"I can handle this case for him."

She probably should have her head examined. Not for offering to handle a simple drunk-and-disorderly charge, but for the direction her thoughts had taken. Morgan Price was the perfect solution to her problem. She needed a favor, and he wanted a criminal lawyer for his employee. Who said the barter system wasn't alive and well, even if this was Los Angeles?

"The firm won't allow it."

She wasn't about to be dissuaded. Not when she finally had a plan capable of resolving her own problem. All she had to do was convince the guy who stirred her senses to agree with her terms. "I'm not talking about the firm, Nick. Me. *I* could do it."

"Were you not in the associates' meeting this morning?" he asked rhetorically. "You can't take on another case and still manage your current caseload, especially since I need you to second-chair two big trials."

Undaunted, she stood and circled the desk. "I can

do it, Nick," she said again, propping her hip against the elegant mahogany. "It's a simple case. It won't take me but a morning or an afternoon out of the office."

Nick regarded her speculatively. "What's in it for you?" he asked.

She shrugged. "I just feel for the guy, that's all," she hedged, wondering if what she was seriously considering breached the wall of ethical legal practices.

Nick stood and looked at her, a slight grin tugging his lips. "Okay, you win. One day, Jill. That's all. And the firm is not to be associated with this case whatsoever. You'll have to do whatever prep work is necessary on your own time."

She smiled, hoping her plan worked. "Thanks, Nick."

His grin was rueful at best. "Don't thank me yet. You wrap this up, and quick."

"I can handle it," she said again, straightening.

"I wouldn't do this for anyone else, Jill. Morgan is a good friend, but he's got a serious problem."

Oh great, she thought and frowned. She was about to proposition a lunatic. "Problem?"

Nick nodded. "Morgan's the quintessential nice guy. He can't say no to anyone in need."

Her frown quickly faded. She'd finally found a solution to her own problem, and in time to fly home to Homer, Illinois for her little sister's wedding at the end of the month.

Morgan Price needed a criminal lawyer.

She needed a fiancé.

And her intended was a guy who couldn't say no.

As far as she was concerned, it was a match made in heaven.

MORGAN COULDN'T get those big sapphire eyes out of his mind. Or that honey-blond hair, swept up into a complicated style that he'd itched to touch and let slide through his fingers. He couldn't remember the last time he'd reacted so strongly to a woman. Especially one he didn't know and doubted he'd ever see again.

He strode through the doors of Price Construction, unable to shake the image of the blue-eyed angel from his mind. She was pretty, he thought, in a cute way. And damned if he couldn't help wondering if she was petite and curvy or long and lithesome. About the only things he did know were there'd been no ring proclaiming her as another's territory, and she'd certainly snagged his attention to the point of heavenly distraction.

Morgan frowned. He had more immediate concerns. Like finding a lawyer for his employee. He'd been called out to another job site and had been in the neighborhood, so driving into downtown Los Angeles to see if his friend Nick could help, hadn't been a complete waste of time.

You're wasting it now, thinking about a woman you'll probably never see again.

Sylvia, his all-around right arm, hung up the phone when he stopped in front of her desk. "Thank heavens you're back," she said, her usually calm voice tinged with exasperation.

"What's wrong now?" Morgan slid a stack of pink slips from the holder, forcing himself to concentrate on business instead of wondering if the angel had long hair that teased her waist.

He flipped through the messages, frowning when he saw "urgent" marked on one from his sister, Raina. Right behind it was one from the business office of the college she attended. Fortunately, a check for her summer tuition and one for her dorm and living expenses had been mailed—something he'd finally taken care of that morning.

Sylvia slipped her pencil behind her ear and looked up at him, her dark brown eyes filled with concern. "The superintendent on the MasCon job has called four times in the past three hours. The guys never came back after lunch, and Dan Castle is fuming, threatening to pull us off the job for good this time if there isn't a stable crew on site first thing in the morning."

Morgan's frown deepened. He didn't need this, not with the huge bonus at stake that MasCon would pay if the job was completed early. Not only could he reward his men for all their hard work, but the extra cash would go a long way toward helping with his brother and sister's college expenses. "Do you know where they are?"

The frown tugging her peppery brows together expressed her own irritation. "They went to see if they could bail Eddie out of jail."

Morgan shoved his hand through his hair and blew out a stream of breath that did little to ebb his growing annoyance. "I told Steve this morning when he called that I was taking care of it."

"When Eddie didn't show up for work by lunch, the guys decided to take matters into their own hands." Sylvia shrugged. "I tried to talk them into waiting, but they feel responsible for what happened to Eddie last night and they wanted to help."

"Son of a—"

The phone rang and Sylvia grabbed it. "Price Construction." Her professional tone conveyed none of her earlier frustration. "Yes, Mr. Castle, he just arrived. One moment please."

She tapped the hold button and gave him a sympathetic grin. "It's Dan Castle. Again."

For all of two seconds, Morgan thought about asking Sylvia to tell Castle the problem would be resolved immediately, but he'd never been one to shirk his responsibilities, and he wasn't about to start now with something as important as the future of his company at stake.

He nodded abruptly and crossed the open space to the small office in the back. Dropping into the chair behind his desk, he took in a deep breath and lifted the receiver, hoping he could placate the job superintendent enough to salvage his company's reputation.

"Hello, Dan," he said, slipping a pen from the drawer. "I just found out about the crew, and I apologize. I'll have the men on site first thing tomorrow."

"Because your guys left, we're now a day and a half behind schedule," Dan Castle roared into the phone. "How do you expect the ceiling crew to install grid or the electricians to do their job if I don't have any walls for them to work with?"

Morgan checked his watch and nearly groaned. It was after five, so offering to send a new crew was useless. "They'll be there, Dan."

"They'd better be. I've got an uptight safety inspector threatening to red-tag the site because some cub installer wore tennis shoes to the job, and this guy's coming back tomorrow. I don't need this kind of aggravation, Price."

"Dan, I promise you, the men will be on the job tomorrow. Six o'clock sharp." And he'd personally ensure they were up to every safety code in the book before they left the shop and headed out to the site. The last thing he needed was for his men to be responsible for a red-tag shutdown. "We'll bring the job in on time. You have my word on it."

"Right now your word doesn't mean a whole hell of a lot," Dan complained.

Morgan cringed. MasCon was an important contract, not only because of the money he'd make on the current project, but he had a half-dozen more big jobs lined up with the general contractor, which would provide his men with steady work well into the following year. If they were pulled from the job and their future contracts canceled, word would spread that Price Construction was unreliable. That was something he couldn't afford, especially with the construction industry in a major slump.

"They'll be there," Morgan said. If he had to personally man the job, he'd do it. It wouldn't be the first time he'd put his tool belt back on to bring a job in on time.

"They'd better be," Dan threatened, "or don't bother coming back. And for every day the job is in the hole, you can bet you'll be hit with the penalties."

Before Morgan could offer a reply, the line went dead. He hung up the phone and scrubbed a hand down his face. God, he didn't need this now.

Sylvia walked into his sparsely furnished office and set another phone message on his desk, this one from a supplier promising to have material delivered to another job site the following day. "Steve just called," she told him, planting her hands on her ample hips. "They managed to bail Eddie out of jail, but the kid's got an arraignment at ten tomorrow morning."

Morgan reached for the phone. He had to call the guys and let them know they needed to be in the shop early. Then he'd let them know that he wasn't happy with the stunt they'd pulled today.

"Don't bother," she said as he flipped through the Rolodex file for Steve's number. "Steve said the four of them won't be at work tomorrow."

"What? I need them on that job, Sylvia." If he had no crew on site as promised, he could kiss the future of Price Construction, and that of his kid brother and sister, goodbye. People were depending on him—not only the family he'd taken care of for as long as he could remember, but there were other drywall carpenters banking on him to keep them from the unemployment lines.

"I told Steve they'd better show," she said. "They're on their way in now to talk to you. Steve said since you didn't get Eddie the lawyer like you promised, the guys are planning to go to court with him in the morning."

"And do what? Plead stupidity for getting Eddie drunk on his twenty-first birthday?" he complained irritably.

Sylvia shrugged, her gaze filled with sympathy. "They feel responsible, Morgan."

"How responsible are they going to feel if we don't have any work?" he muttered, retrieving the telephone book from the bottom desk drawer. How he was going to find a lawyer at this time of the evening, he didn't know.

Twenty minutes later, he shoved the phone book away in disgust. He still hadn't found an attorney willing to take a minor drunk and disorderly charge at the last minute. And he'd only been able to find two lawyers in their offices past five o'clock.

Visions of expressive sapphire eyes and honey-blond hair drifted through his mind unbidden. He needed a miracle. And he couldn't find one if he kept thinking about the blue-eyed angel and wondering if the rest of her was just as inspirational.

MIRACLES CAME in all shapes and sizes, her great-grandmother, Ethel Cassidy, used to tell her great-granddaughters. Jill was convinced her miracle was six foot two with fierce gray eyes and a body made for sin.

She pulled over to the curb to study the guide map again. Most of her time was spent in Los Angeles and the San Fernando Valley, so she was unfamiliar with the Inland Empire and having serious doubts of ever finding Morgan Price's home.

Unwilling to give up hope, she flipped off the overhead light and continued farther up Canyon Crest Boulevard, finally locating the street she'd been searching for for the better part of an hour. After a series of twists and turns on curving and hilly side streets and a couple of cul-de-sacs, she found the house.

Malibu lights illuminated a concrete path from the driveway to the front door of a modest, single-story tract house with a neatly trimmed lawn and a few newly planted evergreens that would eventually grow into decent sized shrubbery. An older model Ford Explorer parked in the driveway in front of a two-car garage and a light shining in the living room window convinced her that her miracle was home. She breathed a sigh of relief that she hadn't driven for two and a half hours through a sea of red taillights for nothing, and cut the engine of her Dodge Intrepid. Pulling her briefcase from the passenger seat, she gathered her courage and marched to the door before she could change her mind.

Jill rang the bell and waited. She had no guarantee that he'd even agree to her terms, and hoped that hint of desperation she'd detected in his eyes had been for real. Mostly, she hoped that Nick was right—that Morgan Price was indeed a guy who couldn't say no to someone in need.

The door swung open and her heart stuttered behind her ribs, followed by an odd unfurling of heat in her middle. The man was simply too handsome for words.

She stared at him like a starstruck fool, paying silent homage to his astonishing good looks. Light spilled onto the porch, and he looked like an avenging angel. His raven-black hair was mussed, giving him a lived-in look she found far too sexy for her peace of mind. Her gaze slipped over him, down the wide chest that tapered to a slim waist she was convinced was as hard as granite, past lean hips and long legs she imagined were powerful and muscular, to bare feet.

Good grief, even his feet were sexy!

"Can I help you?" he asked after her moment of silence.

Her gaze drifted lazily back to his, and she prayed he hadn't seen her reverent inspection of his masculine perfection. Since he hadn't flipped on the porch light, she was hopeful.

"Mr. Price, I'm Jill Cassidy. I'm an attorney from Lowell and Montgomery."

He crossed his arms over his chest and looked down at her, towering well over her five-foot-six height. "Nick have a change of heart?"

He had a pleasant voice, deep and soothing. The kind that would no doubt whisper seductively in a woman's ear and send her pulse careening out of control.

"Not exactly," she said, concentrating on her purpose for coming to see him. "May I come in?"

Relief swept through her when he stepped back to let her into the house. He showed her into a small living room, tastefully but inexpensively furnished.

"Would you like something to drink?" he asked, ushering her toward a blue plaid sofa.

"A glass of water would be nice," she said, smiling up at him.

He nodded absently, then strolled out of the living room, giving her an opportunity to take in her surroundings. A plant in desperate need of attention sat atop an oval end table beside a tall brass lamp. More plants, also lacking tender loving care, were placed on the mantel above a small brick fireplace. Newspapers cluttered the edge of the coffee table, and a collection of magazines were strewn haphazardly beside a worn leather recliner with a remote control resting on the arm.

She eased out a puff of breath. The gods were smiling on her, because her miracle was single. The plants said there might have been a woman in his life at some point. She wasn't planning to have an affair with him; she just needed him to pretend to be her fiancé for a brief period of time.

He returned with her water, then moved to sit across from her on the matching love seat. "So what's this all about? If Nick didn't change his mind, what are you doing here?"

"I can help you, Mr. Price—"

"Morgan," he interrupted, his storm-cloud eyes dipping to her mouth, making her heart beat just a tad faster. "Isn't this a little unusual? I didn't know the partners at Lowell and Montgomery allowed their associates to moonlight."

She smoothed her moist palms down her navy linen skirt. "They don't," she said, offering him a brief smile. "Not as a rule, anyway. I'm not here on behalf of the firm."

He leaned forward and braced his elbows on his knees, giving her a level stare. "Then what are you doing here?"

She set the glass on the coffee table. "Mr. Pr—Morgan. I was hoping we could help each other."

He regarded her skeptically, but the hopeful light in his eyes boosted her waning confidence slightly. "I'm listening," he prompted, his brows pulling into a frown.

"In exchange for my providing legal services for your employee, I'd like something in return."

He didn't say anything, just kept looking at her with those piercing gray eyes.

"I need..."

Oh, why was this suddenly so difficult? She'd planned her speech down to the last detail during her two-hour drive in evening traffic.

"I need a few days of your time," she hedged.

His brows pulled deeper together. "When?"

"The end of the month. My sister is getting married and I need...a...date."

"For a few days?"

She let out a breath that did little to calm her case of nerves. "The wedding is in Illinois. In the town where I grew up."

Regret filled his eyes and her heart sank. "I have to be honest with you, Ms. Cassidy, I'm not sure I can afford—"

"Jill," she said. "And don't worry about the money. I'll pay for everything."

"I'm not sure I can afford to be out of town," he said, leaning back on the love seat and crossing his arms over that gloriously wide chest. He propped his foot on his knee. "I have a business to run."

"Five days," she said, feeling her only hope slipping away. If Morgan Price didn't agree, she didn't know what she was going to do. She'd been evading the issue with her family for months, coming up with one excuse after another as to why her fiancé hadn't been able to come with her on her last two trips back to Homer, Illinois. She hadn't meant to lie to them, but everything had spun out of control and now she was backed into a corner and desperate enough to use whatever means at her disposal to convince Mr. Sinfully Sexy to compound her fabrication.

"A few in exchange for decent legal representation for your employee?" she asked, hating the hesitancy in her voice, but under his piercing stare she was lucky her voice worked properly.

He regarded her with a great deal of caution, and she really couldn't blame him. Her plan was more than ludicrous, it was insane.

"This is blackmail, you know," he said after a moment, his gaze softened by a slight quirk of his mouth.

Relief, combined with a stirring of something much more elemental, rippled through her. "I was thinking more in terms of the medieval economic system. You need a lawyer and I need something in return."

"How do I know you're any good?"

Why did that perfectly innocent question cause gooseflesh to break out all over her skin? "I'm very good. You won't be disappointed."

The grin that transformed his granite features was filled with sin. "You don't leave me much choice."

She smiled and used every ounce of self-control she possessed not to jump up and squeal with delight. "I was hoping you'd say that. So we have a deal?"

"Tell me something. Why resort to blackmailing for a date to a wedding?"

She reached for the water, taking a drink in hopes of putting out the slow burn in her tummy caused by her precedent-setting case of nerves. "Actually," she said, setting the glass back on the table, "I need a little more than just a date."

At his silence, she summoned her nerve and blurted, "I need you to be my fiancé."

2

JILL'S WORDS registered and hung between them, dimming the brightness of his angel's halo. Fool's gold, he thought. And he was an even bigger fool for allowing himself to feel desperate enough that he was seriously considering her outrageous proposal. "You're kidding, right?"

She bit her bottom lip and shook her head slowly. "It's really a very long and boring story," she said, leaning over to pull a yellow pad from her briefcase. She slipped the cap off an expensive pen. "Let's start with the charges against your employee. What's his name?"

"Eddie Burton," he said, then shook his head. "But I haven't agreed yet."

Delicately arched golden brows shot up and her big blue eyes rounded in surprise. "But I thought you needed an attorney?"

"At the cost of selling my soul to get one?" he countered dryly. He didn't have a choice. Of course he'd do whatever she asked, even if it meant he *did* have to sell his soul to keep the MasCon contracts. When the guys had come into the shop earlier that evening, he'd promised them he'd look out for Eddie so long as they showed up for work the next morning.

Confidence and amusement mingled within the

depths of her gaze. Only the quick, rhythmic drumming of her long slender fingers against the legal pad betrayed her nervousness. He found her slight case of anxiety endearing.

"I'm not asking for your soul, Mr. Pr—Morgan. You're not really going to *be* my fiancé, just provide a convincing facsimile. Your time in exchange for competent legal representation. Seems like a fair trade to me."

He wasn't so sure. Time away from the company could cost him a lot more than shelling out a few bucks for a lawyer. Not that spending a few days with her would be a hardship. Quite the opposite, considering his immediate physical reaction when he'd found her on his doorstep.

Therein lay his problem. He was attracted to her, damn attracted when he couldn't afford the distraction, no matter how much awareness rumbled through him whenever she flashed those baby blues his way.

He propped his feet on the edge of the old coffee table and leaned back into the love seat, crossing his arms over his chest. "Let's assume I agree to do this. What exactly are you expecting?"

She set the pad and pen on the table, wrapped her arms around her middle and leaned forward. "We need to be a real couple, one convincing enough that my family doesn't become suspicious."

The ramifications of that statement slammed into him. His imagination tripped through a few dozen ways he'd like to be coupled with her. "Mind telling me why?" he asked, attempting to focus on the conversation and not what she'd look like with her hair down and those delicate hands moving over his body.

Her gaze shifted toward the fireplace, then back again. When she looked up at him, her eyes filled with a despair that nearly had him coming off his seat to offer her comfort.

Not a good sign, he thought with a frown. The last thing he needed to do was get involved with a woman, no matter how enticing. Between running the company, the problems on the MasCon job, and taking care of his kid brother and sister, his cup runneth over.

A light blush stained her cheeks. "So they won't know I've been lying to them for the last seven months," she said quietly.

"Isn't that just a little unethical, even for a lawyer?"

She gave him a wry grin. "I take it you haven't heard that lawyers are notorious for twisting the truth," she said with a quirk of her pink mouth. "Let's just say I'm trying to avoid a complication at home. Your presence will go a long way in helping me achieve that goal."

His frown deepened. "Complication how?"

She blew out a stream of breath that ruffled her wispy honey-gold bangs. "I'm not a bad person," she said, a note of defiance in her tone. "I never *meant* to lie to my family. It was just easier to let them believe there was someone important in my life. I'm a preacher's daughter, which probably means I'll have to spend eternity somewhere hot and sweaty for lying to them. I'm also the first and only Cassidy to ever leave the family fold for the 'wickedness of greener pastures,' as my father says. Another one of my many sins, I'm sure.

"I'm nothing like my sisters," she added, making him wonder if this was another black mark against her. Her words painted a picture of a stern, fire-and-brimstone preacher, more condemning than forgiving.

"That's not so unusual in families," he offered. His sister and brother were more like their intellectual father, while Morgan preferred to work with his hands. He wasn't sure how it had happened, considering the three of them were raised by the same absentee mother. As much as he'd resented his mother's choice of a career over her children when he was growing up, at least he'd inherited her work ethic.

"I'm the sixth of seven daughters, all married except Carly, who's changing her marital status in three weeks." She fidgeted with the hem of her skirt, drawing his gaze to her legs. Legs that had his hands itching, wanting to see if they were as silky smooth as they looked.

"I'm also the only one unattached, serious or otherwise. That alone is an even greater sin according to the residents of Homer," she added, a rueful smile lurking around her mouth when he looked at her again. "My family has been trying to convince me to return to the fold and exchange my career for a husband and my briefcase for a diaper bag. That's not who I am."

Maybe if you took a little more interest—

That's not who I am.

He shut down the memory before it had a chance to

fully surface. He had more immediate concerns than dwelling on a past he couldn't change.

"You haven't thought of telling them what you just told me?" he suggested.

"I've tried. I thought I was making progress until my sister Alison married a year ago. The pressure really started then, but since Carly's gotten engaged, it's been unbelievable. My father is determined to see each of his daughters married to a 'respectable pillar of the community,'" she said, her last words spoken in a mock baritone.

Jill as a rebellious teen, anxious to spread her wings and experience life on her own terms, wasn't difficult to imagine. She had a quick, witty sense of humor, something her fire-and-brimstone father no doubt resented and attempted to oppress.

"What about your mother?" he asked, sensing there was a softer influence somewhere in her past. When he'd been in her office that afternoon venting his frustration on his friend, he'd seen a compassion in her gaze that was unfeigned.

"My mother wouldn't dare offer an opinion contrary to Dad," she said, a hint of distaste in her voice. "She's so...1950s."

"You need to tell them how you feel."

Her expression lined with worry, and she smoothed her hands over her skirt again. "It's not that easy. When I went home for Ali's wedding, all I heard about was how my sisters were all living good, respectable lives. I, on the other hand, am probably seen as one step away from damnation for my wicked, independent ways."

He'd been having some pretty wicked thoughts

himself, from the moment he'd first caught a glimpse of her. Against his will, she'd drifted in and out of his thoughts for the better part of the afternoon. Now that she was seated across from him, the wickedness had escalated to erotic proportions. His angel had propositioned him and he was powerless to resist, thanks to his latest battle with the alligators nipping at his heels. By asking him to pretend to be in love with her, she'd innocently created a dangerous situation. As far as he was concerned, shifting the pretense of lust into passionate reality held enormous appeal, something he wasn't altogether certain the independent lady lawyer would appreciate.

"Don't get me wrong," she continued, drawing his attention back to their conversation. "I love my family, but I don't think I can stand to go through another family gathering with the town parading their single men in front of me like it was a cattle auction. And I don't need to hear how I should settle down and have a passel of kids, or—"

"That still doesn't explain why you told them you were engaged."

"I *didn't* tell them I was engaged," she said, her brows pulling together in a frown. She let out another sigh, this one filled with frustration. "My parents are very traditional, so when Carly and Dean got engaged, my folks hosted an engagement party. I couldn't send my regrets without disappointing my baby sister, but when my own grandmother attempted to fix me up with the grandson of one of her oldest friends, that was enough."

He hid a smile at the outrage tingeing her voice. She obviously perceived the fix-up as a betrayal by her grandmother. "So then you told them you were engaged."

"No. I told Luther that I wasn't interested. I didn't want to hurt his feelings, so I fudged the truth and told him I was already involved, but I meant with my career."

"The demanding mistress," he said, unable to keep the hardness out of his voice.

"One thing led to another," she continued, unaware of his bitterness, "and I couldn't say anything without hurting Luther and possibly damaging a fifty-year friendship between our grandmothers. And then my family assumed..." She let out another frustration-filled puff of breath and leaned back against the cushions. "Suffice it to say, this has turned into a nightmare of epic proportions."

"Tell them the truth," he said. Wasn't the truth always the best path? At least that's what he'd taught Raina and Will.

She dropped her head against the back of the sofa and briefly closed her eyes. "God, I wish I could."

Two things struck him, hard. Jill Cassidy wasn't a liar condemned to purgatory for all eternity, as she believed. He could tell by the simple fact that she had no trouble opening up to him, a virtual stranger. The other was more difficult to face.

He wanted her. He couldn't explain it, but he didn't need to rationalize, analyze or otherwise examine his attraction to her. He'd never been one to dissect his feelings, and he wasn't about to start now. If he wanted something, he went after it, and more often than not, he got exactly what he wanted. The thought of being cast in the role as her fiancé, with all those unconscious touches, secret smiles and the unspoken dialogue between lovers connecting on their own level, held a lot of appeal.

She turned her head slightly to the side and looked at him with those big, clear sapphire eyes he wanted to see filled with heat and need. "I hate lying to my family. Don't get me wrong, I do love them, and the last thing I'd ever want is to hurt them, but to be honest...it's been a relief going home recently without having to worry about the bachelor parade."

He shifted on the love seat and leaned forward. "Have you eaten?"

She glanced at her watch. "I had a pasta salad over eight hours ago. Since we still need to go over Eddie's case, I could do the food thing."

"I don't have anything fancy," he said, rising. "Leftover stew okay with you?"

She stood and smiled. "Lead the way. My stomach's been demanding attention for the past twenty minutes."

He waited while she bent to retrieve her pad and pen. The sight of her very feminine posterior pressing provocatively against her navy linen skirt had his heart ricocheting around in his chest. He looked away before he started drooling like a starving mutt.

"Morgan?"

He dragged his gaze back to her face. Still bent over the table, her delicate hand resting on the legal pad, she looked up at him, her bottom lip trapped between her teeth.

He frowned. "Yeah?"

"Would you mind terribly if I took off my shoes?" she asked, straightening. "It's been a long day."

He shrugged. "Sure, go ahead," he said, figuring her odd request was probably one of those midwestern nuances about a lady in the presence of a gentleman—something his casual, Southern California upbringing couldn't hope to understand.

His smile was strained at best as she slipped off a pair of stylish navy pumps and sighed, curling her toes into the carpet. Her toenails were painted, and he was a sucker for painted toenails. He looked closer and nearly groaned.

Red.

A startling, deep, sensual red.

He was an even bigger sucker for anything red on a woman. Red like fire, representative of the sensual heat women generated when fired up just right.

He blew out a slow stream of breath that did nothing to quell the image of Jill lying before him in a red satin teddy awaiting his pleasure. "This way," he said, then headed into the kitchen, hoping to rein in his runaway erotic fantasies along the way.

She followed and perched on the thin cushion of a bar stool with her legal pad in front of her. "Okay, tell me about Eddie. I'm assuming he's still in custody."

He pulled a large pot from the cabinet. "In a minute," he said, crossing the kitchen to the refrigerator to retrieve the leftover beef stew. No matter how selfish, the last thing he wanted to discuss right now was Eddie's legal problems. He wanted to know more about Jill. Considering the headaches and the frustration Eddie's twenty-first birthday party had cost the company, and him, another few minutes of conversation that would no doubt reveal more about his blackmailing, resourceful angel wouldn't cause a bit more damage.

He dumped the stew into the pot, then set the burner to low. "There's still something I don't understand," he said, crossing back to the refrigerator. He pulled out two sodas, lifting them for her inspection.

She shook her head and tapped her half-full glass of water. "What's that?"

Unspoken dialogue between lovers...

He shook the thought from his mind and concentrated on their verbal communication. "Couldn't you fabricate some reason as to why your fiancé can't make it?"

She started tapping her fingers on the pad again. "Since this entire mess started, I've been home twice, both times with a convenient excuse as to why my intended had to stay behind."

"So what's one more excuse?" he asked, pulling out the bar stool across from her.

"Because the good reverend made it crystal-clear he expected to 'meet my young man.' An auspicious occasion such as Carly's wedding is no doubt the perfect time to inspect and interrogate his future son-in-law."

Morgan knew he was playing with fire by agreeing to her terms, but he really didn't have much choice. He'd promised his men he'd take care of the problem, and he wouldn't disappoint them. "All right," he said, a reluctant grin tugging his lips when hope filled her gaze. "Eddie's being arraigned in the morning. I guess you've got yourself a fiancé."

Her smile was perilous to his central nervous system, and brighter than California sunshine.

She reached across the Formica countertop and settled her hand over his forearm. A current of electricity sparked and sizzled between them. "Thank you, Morgan," she said quietly, a light frown creasing her brow.

Did she feel it, too? he wondered as her fingers slowly slid from his arm. Had she been experiencing that same sensual pull that had been plaguing him since he'd first set eyes on her?

"Yes, well." She looked away and gently cleared her throat. The moment passed, but the truth remained. There was a definite sexual attraction at work. Whether or not they explored the possibilities was another matter altogether. Regardless of how much he wanted the angel with the heavenly body and red polished toenails, one simple fact remained: any carnal liaison they might take pleasure in would be temporary. Jill Cassidy was a career woman, and he'd made the firm resolution years ago to never have a serious, lasting relationship with corporate ladder types.

"About Eddie," she said, her tone and persona shifting from personal to more efficient and business-like. "It's my understanding he's been charged with three misdemeanors. Drunk in public, disorderly conduct, and destruction of private property. Nick also mentioned the property damage is a couple of thousand dollars. Do you know if Eddie has the means to pay the property damage tomorrow?"

Morgan stood to check the stew, providing her with the sketchy details of the impromptu birthday celebration gone awry. "I've already paid the damages," he said, snagging a wooden spoon from the drawer. "This is his first offense. He's a good kid and my best foreman. I'd hate to see one night of poor judgment haunt him for the rest of his life."

She dropped her pen on the pad. "That was extremely generous of you," she said, a gentle smile curving her lips. "Since you've already paid it, there's a good chance I can get the two remaining charges reduced to municipal ordinance violations and a small fine, if not dropped completely. I really need to talk to Eddie, though, since he's my client. Would you mind arranging a meeting for me?"

Morgan returned to the bar and sat. "Tonight? Out of the question."

She crossed her arms and leaned against the back of the bar stool. "Why?"

"He told me he was going to his folks' place for the night, and I don't have their number. I'm meeting him at the courthouse tomorrow morning."

She shrugged, then moved again, shifting in her seat so she could prop her feet on the stool next to her. "Well, unless you have more details for me, I guess that's about it for business until tomorrow morning."

Why that simple statement ignited his imagination, he couldn't be sure, but he moved away from the bar and served up two bowls of stew to gain some distance. After setting one in front of her, he sat, wondering why he didn't feel a greater sense of relief. He'd solved one of his problems by keeping the promise to his men that he'd make sure Eddie had a good lawyer. The men would arrive on the job site at six o'clock sharp, as he'd promised Dan Castle. Yet, instead of the relief he'd expected, another more dangerous emotion continued to jockey for his attention.

Lust for the lady lawyer with the red toenails.

And he was a sucker for a lady in red.

3

JILL HURRIED toward the courthouse, her steps falter-
ing when she spotted Morgan waiting for her. Her
heart did a little flip in her chest, followed by a series
of distinct thumps. The man was simply way too
sexy, and to top it off, he was a great cook. She knew
her way around the kitchen, but working long hours
and living alone didn't provide her with many op-
portunities to enrich her meager talent. Takeout and
instant was about all she had the time or energy for
these days.

And there was just something incredibly seductive
about a man cooking for a woman.

"Good morning," she called to him, surprised that
her voice worked. Something about this guy short-
circuited her senses, common and otherwise, and she
was at a loss to figure out why.

"Good morning," he said in that voice she easily
imagined whispering seductive words against her
ear. Like good morning after a great night!

She came to a stop in front of him and looked up,
struggling to ignore the temptation of those sexy
words her imagination conjured. His eyes were filled
with concern for his employee, touching her heart
and making her melt just a tiny bit. Her boss was
right. Morgan *was* the quintessential nice guy. If she

was seriously in the market for happily-ever-after, Morgan Price would no doubt be at the top of her list as a prime candidate.

"Good news," she told him, flashing him a grin she couldn't have stopped even if her life was in jeopardy. He just did that to her. "Since you already paid for the damages Eddie caused, the bar owner has dropped the charges, so the only th..." She looked around, then back at Morgan. "Where *is* Eddie?"

"Inside," Morgan said, taking her elbow and steering her in the direction of the glass doors. "Waiting and scared."

He led her toward a wooden bench where a young man dressed in neatly pressed jeans, plaid shirt and solid blue tie waited, his foot tapping nervously on the tile floor. As they approached, he stood, his pale blue gaze darting from her to Morgan and back again.

The first thing Jill noticed was the worry lining his features. The second was that Eddie Burton looked as if he'd be more comfortable in a lab dissecting frogs than getting roaring drunk and tearing up a neighborhood tavern. A shock of carrot-red hair was cut in a cropped style. His eyebrows were pulled together in a frown, wrinkling his heavily freckled forehead.

Morgan introduced them, and Jill shook Eddie's hand, smiling in hopes of setting him at ease. "It's not all that bad," she told both men. "The bar owner has dropped the charges, but there's still the D&D charge to deal with."

"Am I going to jail again?" Eddie asked, the fear in his eyes and his voice all too real. She thought of Nick's advice to let the public defender's office han-

dle the case. Considering the workload of the jaded
public counsel, the chances of Eddie doing time, even
if it was only a day or two, could have been very real.
There was no way she was going to allow this fright-
ened young man to spend another minute in custody.

"No. You won't go to jail," she told him firmly, setting her briefcase on the bench. "The judge may order
you to serve a probationary period or perhaps just
some community service, but that's if we actually do
go to trial."

"What happens today?" Morgan asked.

"Today is only the arraignment," she said, then
turned her attention back to Eddie. "The judge will
ask you how you plead, and I want you to say not
guilty. He'll assign a trial date, and that's all there is
for today."

Eddie wouldn't look at her. He stared down at the
tips of his highly polished boots, instead. "But I did
it," he murmured so softly she had a difficult time
hearing him.

"That's okay," Jill explained, "but I don't want you
telling that to anyone other than me, okay?"

When Eddie nodded, she continued. "The reason
you plead not guilty is to give me time to establish a
defense and to try to get the district attorney to drop
or lessen the charges against you."

"Defense?" Morgan asked, his tone incredulous.
"You think it'll go that far?"

"It's possible," she said, shifting her gaze to him.
He raked a hand through his black-as-midnight hair,
which looked as if he'd been finger-combing it for
hours. "I won't know for certain until Eddie and I get
a chance to talk about what happened that night."

She settled her hand on Morgan's forearm and tried to ignore the sparks of electricity shooting up her arm and spreading throughout her body with lightning speed. "Your paying the bar owner made a difference. It's just a matter of me convincing the prosecution to drop the rest of the charges," she said, concentrating on the case and not the way her breasts tingled and rasped against the satin cups of her bra.

"Can you really do that?" Eddie asked, the hopeful note in his voice drawing her attention.

"I'll know more later," she reassured him, letting her hand slip from Morgan's arm. "You and I will need to talk first. Is there somewhere we can meet?"

"My office," Morgan said. "Later this afternoon."

Jill shook her head. "I can't. I have—"

"Excuse us a minute, Eddie." Morgan took her arm and steered her a few feet away.

"Am I or am I not paying for legal representation for my employee?"

Jill frowned at the authoritative tone of his voice. "In a manner of speaking, yes, you are. But that doesn't mean you can—"

"I'd prefer it if you met with him at my office." Determination replaced his earlier concern, which didn't surprise her. From what she'd seen of his personality thus far, determination was one of his more mild qualities. Sexual magnetism ranked at the top.

"But I don't see—"

"I need him on the job, Jill. Today. He'll be back at the shop by four-thirty. Meet with him then, and hopefully you'll have this mess wrapped up in a few days."

"It might not be that easy." She had more pre-trial

motions Nick was expecting, and he'd made it perfectly clear that she could handle this case for Morgan only if it didn't interfere with her own caseload.

"You said—"

"I know what I said," she told him, lowering her voice slightly, "but Eddie's scared to death and I'm trying to set him at ease." She glanced in her client's direction. He'd returned to the bench and was again nervously tapping his boot on the tile. "It all depends on who's been assigned from the D.A.'s office. If we get a seasoned A.D.A., I can probably have the case dismissed. But, if we get a recent grad anxious for some trial experience..."

Morgan's frown deepened. Dammit. He'd hoped one morning of his time away from work was all that'd be necessary, but if Jill was right, that could change. "Over something so ridiculous," he complained. And costly, he added silently.

"I've seen worse." She stepped around him and walked back to where Eddie waited. Morgan watched her go, enjoying the gentle sway of her hips beneath the fabric of the short teal skirt that enhanced the length of her legs. She wore a pair of black pumps that hid her brightly colored nails, and he found himself wishing she'd worn those strappy kind of shoes that showed off the delicate structure of a woman's foot.

She said something to Eddie, checked her watch, then looked over her shoulder at him and motioned toward the open courtroom door.

He followed them into the crowded, wood-paneled courtroom and took the vacant seat directly behind her and Eddie. Her hair was swept up in that complicated style again, giving him no hint as to the length of all that silky honey trapped within the confines of a clawlike gadget. The urge to reach over and unclip her hair and let it fall around her shoulders nearly overwhelmed him.

He leaned forward and breathed in her scent, a beguiling floral mix that awakened his libido. "Is that the A.D.A?" he asked in a hushed whisper.

She glanced in the direction he indicated and nodded before turning slightly in her chair to look at him. Those big blue eyes captured his, and for reasons that defied common sense, a flicker of heat shot south.

This woman was trouble.

"Technically," she said in a hushed businesslike tone, "but she's probably a relatively new lawyer. They use them as arraignment clerks, and it's not likely she'll be the attorney ultimately assigned to the case. These type of proceedings are pretty rote, so there's not much risk of a screwup at this stage."

Oh yeah, he thought. Big trouble, since he couldn't seem to drag his gaze away from her peach-tinted lips. Major trouble, he amended, since he'd spent the night tossing and turning in his king-size bed thinking about her.

He tried to push those thoughts aside and make a mental list of things he needed to cover today, but his traitorous conscience refused to heed his wishes. He tried to pay attention to the various proceedings ahead of theirs, but the beguiling scent of her subtle perfume wafted toward him, making his synapses misfire like an old Chevy in need of a tune-up.

Ninety minutes later, the clerk called Eddie's

name. Jill rose and stepped across the bar, holding the low swinging door for Eddie to follow.

"Jill Cassidy, your honor, counsel for defendant, Edward Burton," she said briskly, setting her briefcase on the table.

Morgan leaned forward and braced his elbows on his knees, paying close attention to the proceedings, and Jill. The sweetness he'd witnessed thus far evaporated, and she was all business. Real cool, too, he noted as she requested in a firm, professional manner that the charges against Eddie for property damage be officially dismissed.

In a matter of minutes it was over, just as she'd predicted. With a little legal double-talk she managed to hold the trial over for three months, waive a jury and get the court to refund half of the bail money.

Morgan was impressed.

And disappointed.

For as much as Jill Cassidy interested him as a woman, continually setting off a series of sparks inside him whenever he thought about her, she was as off-limits as a woman could be, as far as he was concerned. He had nothing against professional women. He supported equal pay for equal jobs and a woman's right to choose, but when it came to lasting relationships, a woman with a briefcase could be nothing more to him than a brief affair. Too bad *he* wasn't the type to embark upon a casual fling, because he didn't doubt for a nanosecond they could really have a great time together.

No, he decided. Despite his attraction to her, it really was best that he keep his distance, emotionally and otherwise. Once he'd repaid his debt to her for taking on Eddie's case, that would be the end of his association with Jill. He owed her for helping him out of a jam that could have cost his budding company thousands of dollars. There could be nothing else between them.

He stood as Jill and Eddie walked toward him, a twinge of regret shifting through him. He liked her, a lot. When he was a kid he'd learned that career women and family had about as much in common as fire and water. Further confirmation followed him into adulthood, and it was a good thing. Otherwise, a woman like Jill, with her hundred-watt smile, her intellectual wit and enough sex appeal to tempt a Benedictine monk, could really get under his skin and wrap herself around his heart.

Yeah, he thought, falling into step behind her as she inclined her head toward the door, a woman like Jill definitely had heartbreaker written all over her.

The problem was, he had a bad feeling she was about to become his favorite reading material.

JILL STEPPED OUT into the warm June sunshine, promising to meet Eddie later that afternoon to go over the details of his case, then waited while Morgan issued him a set of instructions for a job.

She checked her watch. The other proceedings had taken much longer than she'd expected, and it was nearly noon. Driving the sixty miles back to the Wilshire District made little sense when she'd only have to turn around and come right back. Luckily, she'd brought work home the previous night, and she decided she could put the time away from the office to good use at a local law library by making some headway on those motions Nick was expecting.

"You wouldn't happen to know where the law library is, would you?" she asked Morgan once Eddie left. "I have some work that I need to do."

They walked down Ninth toward Main, where she'd parked her car. "I'm not sure, but it's probably in San Bernardino," he said, taking hold of her elbow when they stepped off the curb. "The area's kinda rough, though. I'd feel more comfortable if you used my office."

Those darned electric tingles skittered up her arm and shot down to her tummy. If she didn't get a grip, by the time they returned from Homer she'd be nothing more than an incinerated mass.

"So what happens now?" he asked, after they crossed the street.

The length of his tanned fingers, still wrapped seductively around her elbow as he walked her toward her car, sent little shock waves of pleasure over her skin. "After I talk to Eddie," she said, "I'll need to contact the prosecutor and discuss the case. Eddie's a good kid, and this should easily go away for him. He might have to do community service or maybe probation, but that's about it."

She stopped and set her purse on the hood of her car to look for her keys.

"This your car?" Morgan asked, a note of caution in his voice.

She found her keys and looked up at him and the frown tugging his brows. She glanced at her car, and her heart sank. "Oh no," she said, walking to the rear passenger side to examine the flat tire.

"I've changed a flat or two in my time," he said, coming to stand beside her.

Jill couldn't believe her rotten luck. "Normally, I'd take you up on your very generous offer, but this is my spare." She'd gotten a flat a week ago and hadn't had the time to have the tire repaired or replaced. What was it her grandmother had said about putting off today, or some other cliché about the evils of procrastination?

Morgan crouched to examine the tire. "Here's the culprit," he said, pointing to a long, rusty nail sticking out of the rubber. "You picked up a nail."

She pulled her cell phone from her purse and pressed the call button. The LCD panel remained blank. She pressed the button again. Still nothing. "It's dead. I can't believe this is happening."

Morgan straightened. "I've got one in my truck. Come on. You can call from there, then we'll grab a bite to eat across the street while we wait."

"I don't understand," she said, pressing the button again and again while falling into step beside Morgan. "It was working fine this morning."

"Welcome to the electronic age," he said in good humor, pulling his keys from the pocket of his khaki trousers.

He opened the door for her and she set her briefcase on the floorboard. "It's better than the alternative," she said, gauging the height of the truck in comparison to her short, teal silk skirt. "I didn't see a pay phone for the last two blocks."

She frowned, wondering how she was going to climb inside the four-wheel drive. She turned and braced her hands on the seat, prepared to lift herself backward into the truck.

Morgan stepped forward and placed his hands on her hips. She sucked in a sharp breath. The feel of his large hands gripping her hips set off dozens of sensual images. She looked up into his eyes and her breath caught. The hint of desire swirling in the depth of his gaze sent her feminine senses into an uproar.

He moved closer, trapping her between the thick wall of his chest and the interior of his four-wheel drive. Heat surrounded her from head to toe, but not the kind caused by the warmth of the sun. This kind of heat had nothing to do with weather, and everything to do with sex.

As if she weighed no more than one of the sheets of drywall he probably tossed around on a daily basis, he gently lifted her into the truck. She couldn't move. She sat with her feet dangling out the open door, unable to tear her gaze from his, shocked by the strength of her physical reaction and a conscious need to kiss him. One of those deep, tongue-tangling kisses that would have her heart pounding like the thunder of a summer storm.

"Thank you, Jill," he said, a lopsided grin on the lips she couldn't seem to stop fantasizing about. "For everything you've done today."

What was he thanking her for? she wondered. She hadn't even kissed him yet.

He stepped back to close the door. Realization dawned, bringing with it a wave of embarrassment. "Uh, no problem," she said, shifting in the seat, hoping the heat infusing her body was from the warmth of the sun and not because she was turning a very unattractive shade of scarlet.

He closed the door and walked around the front of the truck to climb inside. She slipped her sunglasses from her purse, trying to decide which was the lesser of two evils: confessing the truth to her family that she was still painfully single, or spending time with a man who had her thinking sins of the flesh weren't quite the sacrilege her father preached to his daughters.

MORGAN HEFTED the last sheet of drywall onto the bed of the delivery truck. He'd been hiding out in the small warehouse for the past couple of hours in the futile hope that some distance from Jill would draw his mind away from her sweet, sultry smile.

Not a chance.

He'd hoped the physical labor would distract him from the need clawing his gut whenever she flashed those baby blues his way.

Impossible.

"No way," he grumbled, especially since he couldn't stop wondering if she'd taste as sweet as he'd been imagining all afternoon.

"She's a career woman," he complained, then headed into the humidity of the warehouse for some rope. "That means look, but don't touch."

What had he been thinking? he mused, kicking aside a box filled with drywall screws. Inviting her to spend the afternoon at his office had to qualify as one of his less-than-brilliant ideas.

Her perfume had distracted him.

The soft rasp from the slide of her nylons as she shifted in the chair had ignited his imagination.

The sound of her fingertips gently tapping the keyboard of her laptop computer had him staring at her hands and thinking all sorts of illicit thoughts.

He'd been chased out of his own suddenly cramped office, self-condemned to the heat of the afternoon because avoiding Jill was preferable to the erotic fantasies that kept erupting every time he looked at her, heard her or caught a whiff of her heavenly scent.

The woman and her hundred-watt smile were more trouble than a by-the-book city inspector. The last thing he needed was trouble, especially the kind Jill Cassidy, Attorney-at-Law, represented. She was the last woman on earth he should want to get involved with, but damned if he didn't find her just a little too fascinating and sensual.

He located a bundle of rope and headed back into the brutal sunshine. What was it about her that got to him? he wondered, slapping the rope over the drywall to secure the load to the truck bed. He hardly knew her, but he had a feeling he'd probably figure out how to consistently pick the winning lottery numbers before he had an answer to *that* question. All he had to do was gaze into those expressive eyes and he was a goner.

Chump that he'd become in the past twenty-four hours, he'd done a whole lot of gazing over lunch waiting for the tow truck to arrive.

The back door leading to the offices creaked. He didn't have to look up to know it was Jill. Awareness crackled around him like a live wire as the heels of her black pumps clicked over the concrete floor and onto the blacktop of the alley.

"The tire shop just phoned to tell me my car's ready," she called out. "I was going to get a cab but your secretary said you weren't busy."

"I'll be done in a minute," he answered, making a shipper's knot and tugging hard on the rope. He crouched to loop the rope around the tie-down and froze. The staunch reminder that career women were off-limits faded into the background at the sight of Jill's shapely legs. Legs he wanted to touch, to slide his hands over, to feel wrapped around...

He muttered a muffled curse and tugged on the rope.

"Good grief, it's hot," she said. She moved and he watched with fascination as those legs slowly came around to his side of the delivery truck. "Is it always like this in the valley?"

She crouched beside him and peered beneath the flatbed. The delicate floral of her perfume wafted over him, and his hands stilled as he imagined the daring places she may have dabbed the intoxicating scent. The weather wasn't the only thing heating up—his temperature was skyrocketing.

He turned to look at her. "Not always," he said, deciding it was all her fault. If her eyes didn't sparkle when she cast him one of those sultry smiles, then maybe the rush of need and a deep-in-his-bones desire to kiss her wouldn't be so overwhelming.

He straightened and tossed the rope over the top of the truck to finish tying off the load. There was no way he would be able to spend five days alone with her without kissing her. They were supposed to be engaged. They would be expected to kiss, to touch, to— No, he wouldn't go there.

Maybe he should just kiss her and get it out of the way now.

Yeah, that's it, he thought, picking up the rope and making another knot in the line. Just kiss her, solve the mystery and then she'd be out of his system.

He hoped.

Tossing the rope over the truck again, he circled the back and stopped in front of her. She looked up and smiled, causing his heart to beat heavily in his chest. He stared at her, not sure what to say, and her honey-gold eyebrows puckered into a frown.

"Did you want something?" she asked, her voice filled with curiosity.

"I have to taste you," he admitted, planting his hands on his hips.

The frown smoothed and her eyes darkened to midnight. He'd been afraid something like this would happen. The chemistry between them had been evident from the moment he first laid eyes on her. That churning-in-his-gut feeling was back—a loud and clear warning that his short-circuiting brain wouldn't heed.

She wanted him to kiss her.

Her gaze slipped over him, slowly running down the length of his body. He felt her eyes like a physical caress, all too real and way too tempting.

"You make it sound like it's a bad thing," she said, a smile easing across her peach-tinted lips.

"It is," he said, narrowing the space between them. "It's real bad."

"Bad can be very good, you know," she said in a

husky tone that had his already skyrocketing temperature spiking.

He settled his hand on her hip and rocked her slightly closer. "Just one taste," he said, pressing his fingers against the gentle swell of her hip. He lowered his head until he felt her breath fan his lips.

Her lashes fluttered closed and she breathed in deeply.

And then a pickup truck pulled into the alley.

Morgan dropped his hand and stepped away from her. She looked up, her gaze filled with curiosity, and a hint of disappointment, as well.

"The guys are here," he said, shoving a hand through his hair.

"Too bad," she said, giving him one of those dazzling grins.

Too bad? How about too close?

Or not close enough?

He didn't want to think about the answer, or the disappointment he'd glimpsed in her gaze.

And he especially didn't want to think about the way she'd felt under his hand. All soft, all woman, and all his for the taking.

4

JILL SLIPPED another dusty, obscure volume of the *California Reporter* from the top shelf of the firm's extensive law library. That morning the Martinez trial had taken a left turn neither she or Nick had seen coming, nor been prepared to counter. After a long debate between counsel out of the presence of the jury, the judge had ordered a recess until Monday morning, hopefully giving her and Nick enough time to find the appropriate points and authorities to quash the prosecution's evidence. However, she was beginning to have serious doubts that any amount of midnight-oil research would help.

She added another volume to the one already tucked beneath her arm and climbed down the wooden ladder. She carried the heavy books to the conference room she'd commandeered as a temporary work station and dropped them on the table with a loud thud next to her current towering stack. After a quick glance at the elegant clock above a mahogany armoire, she sighed. Morgan was picking her up at her apartment at seven for dinner, which gave her only three hours of research time if she hoped to shower and change.

She considered calling him and canceling, but decided against it. They needed to establish their rules of engagement sooner or later, and she'd rather give him time to digest and memorize the little details that would make a difference in everyone believing they were the real thing. She'd have to come into the office on the weekend anyway, which also meant her planned shopping trip to buy a new dress for Carly's wedding would be postponed again. Neither task could be put off for much longer, since she and Morgan were scheduled to fly out of LAX early next Wednesday morning for their stay in Homer as the convincing, loving couple.

Five days of lying to her family, with Morgan Price as her phony fiancé pretending to be madly in love with her.

She frowned and flipped through the index of one volume of case law. She hadn't seen Morgan since he'd nearly kissed her, but that didn't mean he hadn't been foremost in her thoughts over the past ten days.

Twice she'd been forced to cancel their scheduled dinner meetings. The first time he'd been understanding. The last time she'd detected a note of annoyance in his deep velvet voice, despite her apologies that last-minute trial preparations were going to keep her in the office much later than she'd expected.

She shrugged. They weren't involved. They weren't even dating. They'd made a bargain, an oral barter contract that didn't contain a clause stating he had a right to be irritated, annoyed or even displeased if she failed to keep an appointment. No man, especially a pretend fiancé, had *that* right.

It wasn't as if she was avoiding him. So what if she'd experienced an unexpected rush of desire when they'd nearly kissed. Just because she'd been filled with a disappointment she hadn't anticipated when their kiss had been thwarted by the arrival of his employees, didn't mean a thing, other than she was wildly attracted to him.

"Like that's a big secret," she muttered, sliding her finger down the index in search of a particular appellate court case. Since the day she'd first hatched her scheme, she hadn't denied she found him to be one sexually appealing specimen.

I have to taste you.

His words drifted through her mind with the same clarity as the day he'd uttered them. A shiver touched her skin now, just as it had when he'd huskily whispered his desire. The hint of need in his voice had made her palms sweat and her toes curl.

She let out a long, gusty sigh. *I am* not *avoiding him,* she told herself firmly, snapping the useless volume closed. The fact that she found him incredibly attractive and a whole lot sexy meant nothing other than her feminine senses were crazily in tune to him. A blushing virgin she was not. Nor was she interested in anything beyond their employment of the medieval economic system. Just because she'd had to cancel a couple of dates—no, not dates, meetings—did not mean she was afraid of the way he made her feel.

"I don't run away from anything or anyone," she muttered to herself. She slid another old volume of case law from the stack and flipped it open to the index. She prided herself on her ability to make decisions and carry them out with precision.

So why are you lying to your family?

Her frown deepened, and she decided to ignore her conscience and those pesky thoughts about spending time with a man who made her pulse race and her knees weak. She needed to stay focused on the case and concentrate on keeping her client's backside out of the slammer.

For her client's sake, the last thing she needed to do was spend hours wondering if Morgan's kisses were half as exciting as the anticipation of his lips pressing against hers.

MORGAN WAITED outside Jill's apartment building until half-past. He was as forgiving as the next guy, and knew from experience that work sometimes interfered with the social calendar, but being stood up for the third time in a row was just a little too much, even for him. By the time he decided to drive across town to her office after a quick stop at a nearby deli, he'd almost convinced himself the need to see her had nothing whatsoever to do with the fact that he hadn't been able to get her out of his mind, but only with their plans for the upcoming week.

They had a deal, and she'd more than kept up her end by managing to have the other two charges against Eddie dropped without so much as an additional fine. In exchange for her legal expertise, he'd promised to play the part of her intended. He couldn't very well carry off the role of doting fiancé if they didn't at least rehearse their script.

He pulled into the deserted parking garage of the downtown high-rise and drove up to the fourth level to the firm's reserved parking area. With a frown, he pulled in beside Jill's car. He had no idea what had kept her in the office this time, but he seriously doubted she'd stopped long enough to eat, let alone call to tell him she couldn't make their date—again.

He stepped through the unlocked doors of Jill's office, past the empty reception area to follow the path of light spilling from a conference room.

The irritation he'd been harboring for the past hour faded away when he found her seated at a long mahogany table.

Volumes, too numerous to count, surrounded her in piles of at least three or four high. Another half dozen lay open over the polished table. Yellow note pads were scattered around an open file filled with legal documents. Her back was to him as she read the book propped in her lap. She'd removed her shoes and her feet were resting on the cushion of another chair, those polished toenails painted a vibrant pink this time, peeking through the tanned shade of her nylons.

Even surrounded by the very reason they could never have a lasting relationship, he still thought she was one of the most beautiful and sensual women he'd ever met. She was the reason medieval knights stormed castle walls. And for five days and *nights*, she'd be his.

She'd rolled up the sleeves of her white silky blouse, and from his position by the door, it looked as if she'd pulled it from the confines of the waistband of a short black skirt hiked high on her thigh, giving him plenty of leg to admire.

But his angel's hair was loose, something he'd fantasized about more than he should. The silky strands floated past her shoulders in a cloud of soft waves. He wanted to touch it, to let that gold silk glide through his fingers, to bury his hands in the soft mass and...

His hand clenched, crinkling the brown paper bag he held.

She looked up, surprise and pleasure mingling in her gaze. A look that went straight to his heart and gave it a distinct tug.

She was pleased to see him.

For the life of him, he couldn't get past that telling sparkle in her gaze or the smile on her lovely face, even if she had stood him up again.

She's a career woman, he firmly reminded himself, and therefore off-limits.

His mind acknowledged the truth.

His heart suffered from serious denial.

His body didn't give a rip!

Confusion suddenly filled her expressive blue eyes, followed by a frown when she glanced down at her thin gold wristwatch. She set the book on the table with the others and stood. "Morgan, I am so sorry," she said, coming around the conference table in her stocking feet. "We had a crisis during the trial. I've got tons of research to do, and I completely lost track of time."

"I can see that," he said, stepping more fully into the room. He shouldn't be bothered that she'd blown him off without a thought. They weren't in the middle of a relationship. Still, it rankled that he could be so easily forgotten. Especially since she was never far from his mind.

She gave him a look filled with guilt. "I apologize. I should have called you."

"I was in the neighborhood," he said, a tiny surge

of satisfaction rising at the contrition in her voice. "Don't worry about it. Hungry?"

She flashed him one of those hundred-watt grins capable of fueling his fantasies. "Starved," she admitted. "Whatever that is, it smells heavenly."

She was heavenly. "I figured something probably came up, and took a chance that you hadn't eaten," he told her, setting the sack on the table. "Since you can't seem to make it to dinner, I thought I'd bring dinner to you."

Her grin was wry. "I am sorry, Morgan. We got hit with a character issue, and the D.A. is trying to put my client's juvenile record before the jury. It's a touchy issue, and we only have until Monday morning to convince the judge to suppress the record."

He shrugged as if her apology wasn't necessary. Except it was, and that bothered him. "I thought juvenile records were sealed once you turned eighteen."

She pulled out a dark-gray leather chair and sat, indicating for him to do the same. "They are, but there are exceptions for when those records can be put into evidence. My client's on trial for misappropriation of funds from a nonprofit organization. He's an upstanding member of his community, and we've used his stellar character as a part of our defense. Unfortunately, he has a past we knew nothing about, one that includes another breach of trust issue, so the judge could allow it."

"Now you've got to do a lot of backpedaling to keep the D.A. from introducing it as evidence."

She nodded and leaned back in the chair. "Very good," she said with a grin. "And a lot of research.

Nick thinks there's some obscure case law we can use in our argument."

He slid the bag holding their dinner toward her. "Pastrami on rye or roast beef and Swiss on squaw bread?"

"Pastrami." She peeked into the bag. "And potato salad?" she asked, a hopeful note in her voice.

"Macaroni and potato, just to be safe."

She pulled the sandwiches and salads from the bag. "I like that in a man," she said, and stood.

He chuckled and watched her cross the conference room to a small refrigerator built into the armoire. "Late nights are common around here," she said, bending forward to peer into the fridge. "Soda, beer or—" she turned and grinned "—we could really be brazen and bust open a bottle of Cabernet."

"Whatever you're having," he said, unable to tear his gaze away from her delectable backside pressing evocatively against the material of her skirt.

She pulled two bottles of beer from the fridge. "It's been a long week," she said, handing him the bottles to open.

Unspoken gestures.

The thought haunted him as he twisted off the caps. Jill was the last woman he should be so in tune to, but briefcase and power suits be damned. He wanted her.

She found paper plates and napkins before returning to the table. "How's your week been?" she asked while serving up their meal.

Morgan took the pickle she offered. "Busy," he said. "Thanks to your keeping Eddie out of jail, it looks like the MasCon job is going to come in on time. Thank you, Jill."

She shrugged. "Just doing my part." She bit into the warm pastrami and closed her eyes. "This is so good," she said after a moment.

"Speaking of parts," he said, after sampling the macaroni salad, "don't you think we should discuss—"

"Ah...our engagement."

"Something like that."

She set her sandwich aside and took a delicate sip of beer. "All we need to worry about is making sure my family and friends believe we're really engaged."

He finished off the small container of salad and reached for his sandwich. "Then I'll need to know more about you."

She nodded. "And I you. What do you want to know?"

Everything.

He shrugged and took a long drink from the bottle of cold beer. "I've got a kid sister, so I know what women are like when they get together."

Understanding lit her gaze. She reached across the table for one of her yellow legal pads. "And they'll want to know everything about *you*," she said, stretching for her pen. "An interrogation that would make the FBI proud, knowing them."

Morgan's heart slammed into his ribs. Her skirt inched up, exposing slim thighs that had him fighting to control the urge to smooth his hand up the back of her leg. "Exactly," he said when she sat again and he found his voice. "So, tell me. What do you know about me?"

"You own your own business. A drywall company."

"How long have I been in business for myself? How did I get into construction?"

Jill groaned good-naturedly and shifted in the chair. Since this little venture into "getting to know you" would undoubtedly take some time, she tucked her legs beneath her to get more comfortable. "Give me the *Reader's Digest* version of The Morgan Price Story," she instructed, pen poised over the legal pad. "My curious sisters will be dying for every last detail since I've been absolutely silent about the fictitious man in my life. Have you always lived in California?"

"My mom moved us here when I was twelve. My parents divorced," he said with a touch of iciness in his voice. "It wasn't friendly."

Jill noticed the hardness in his eyes and voice and filed it away for later inspection. "Who's 'us'?" she asked him, despite her curiosity about the relationship with his parents. "You said something about a sister."

"You've been paying attention," he said with a slight quirk to his lips. "Raina's about to start her last year of college. Will heads to Ohio State in the fall."

"Did you go to college?"

"For a while," he answered. "Shortly after my mom remarried."

Jill caught a hint of something going on behind that steely gaze. She couldn't see a No Trespassing sign posted, but sensed a definite detour. "You dropped out?" she asked carefully.

His hands loosely cupped the amber bottle, and he traced the outline of the label with his thumb. He remained silent, making her wonder if he would give her a more personal glimpse into his past.

He took a deep breath and looked at her. "My mom passed away so I dropped out of school," he explained. The resignation in his voice told her he'd come to terms a long time ago with his aborted plans. "I came home to look after Raina and Will and took the first job I could find. I had worked summers for a construction outfit in Arizona during college, so I landed a full-time job with a drywall company in Orange County."

"What about your father?"

A sadness filled his eyes and he shook his head slightly. "My father had died a couple years before."

Her heart gave a tiny lurch. "I'm sorry," she said quietly.

He shrugged and took a long pull of beer. "It was a long time ago," he finally said.

"What about your stepfather?"

"Raina and Will are my responsibility."

"How old were they?"

"Raina was sixteen when Mom died, and Will was only thirteen."

"You raised your brother and sister?" That explained his need to take care of people, like Eddie Burton.

"It was either me or the court system." He leaned back into the chair. "I wasn't about to let that happen to them."

Whether his caretaker mentality was a trait of the oldest sibling, or just something about Morgan that made him so special, she couldn't be sure. She suspected special. "What did you study in college?" she asked him, more out of curiosity than any attempt to change the subject.

"Mechanical engineering."

She grinned. "I'm impressed."

"Don't be," he said with an answering chuckle. "It's an easy degree for someone who prefers to work with his hands."

She didn't buy that for a minute. He was no slouch in the intellectual department. He ran a business, and from what she'd seen the afternoon she'd spent in the offices of Price Construction, it was a small but successful one. "What did your parents do?"

He settled further back into the leather chair and stretched those long legs in front of him. Unable to help herself, her gaze dipped to his strong thighs and down the length of his denim-covered legs and back up again. Large, long, powerful. All adjectives to describe the man she found irresistible.

The urge to touch him, to see if he really was as marble-hard as she imagined, overwhelmed her. She bit her lip and stuffed the tempting thought in the back of her mind.

"Dad was a literature professor at Ohio State," he said, drawing her gaze reluctantly back to his. She stalled at his mouth. So sexy, she thought.

I have to taste you.

Were those his words she kept hearing, or her own? She didn't know any longer.

"My mother was an advertising executive," he told her. "Will and Raina got Dad's brains. I ended up with my mother's work ethic."

That bitterness crept back into his voice, capturing her attention. "Hard work isn't anything to be ashamed of," she said, setting the pen aside. She didn't need to take notes. She'd never forget a single word he told her about his past.

He shrugged. "What about you?" he asked, firmly changing the subject. "Any old boyfriends waiting back in Homer that I'm going to have to worry about?"

She looked away. "No one important," she lied, not wanting to delve into her past any more than he did.

"You sure?" he asked with a perception that surprised her.

She debated, wondering how much she should tell Morgan about her past. Small towns being what they are, the chances of someone mentioning Owen Kramer to Morgan were relatively high. "Just one," she reluctantly confessed. "You don't have to worry about him. Owen Kramer is ancient history, married with a couple of kids now."

She shuddered at the thought of her narrow escape.

He folded his hands over his lean belly and gave her a level stare. "Was it serious?"

She drummed her fingers on the legal pad and let out a long, steady breath. "I was engaged once upon a time."

His dark eyebrows hiked in curiosity. "What happened?"

I opened my eyes.

"It didn't work out."

Morgan regarded Jill carefully. It seemed the lady lawyer had her own secrets she wasn't willing to share, something he understood all too well. "Your choice or his?" he asked.

She stood and cleared away their dinner. "Mine," she said, stuffing the bag with their used paper plates and napkins.

"Sounds interesting," he prompted.

"It's not," she said crisply. She carried the bag to the garbage can in the corner and tossed it inside. "Our parents were all for the marriage and very disappointed when I called it off. That should tell you something."

It didn't, not really. Something had happened, and from Jill's reaction, he'd bet the breakup had been anything but friendly. He suspected that if he were foolish enough to get involved with her, *which he was not*, letting go of Jill Cassidy wouldn't be all that simple. She was the kind of woman who would definitely leave her mark on a guy's heart for a very long time. She was sweet, smart and sexy. A lethal combination.

He sensed her shifting mood and quickly changed the subject, not wanting their evening to end too soon. He asked her a few impersonal questions and exchanged other statistical information with her.

An hour and a half later, Morgan glanced at his watch and stood. Even if he hadn't been able to take Jill to the quiet, romantic Italian restaurant he'd planned, he reluctantly admitted he'd enjoyed their evening together. His intent had been to get to know her better, and he hadn't been disappointed. "I should probably get out of here and let you get back to work."

"I doubt I'll get any more research done tonight,"

she said as she stood. "Calling it a night sounds like a good idea."

He waited while she organized her books and notes into several neat piles then slipped back into her black pumps. She reached across the table for the clawlike clip and started twisting the length of her hair into a knot.

"Leave it down," he said, hating to see all that beautiful silk hidden from view.

She gave him an odd look, then shrugged before circling the table. "Where are you parked?" she asked, leading the way out of the conference room and down the hallway into the offices.

"Next to your car," he said, following her into her private office. Behind her desk, framed diplomas and certificates granted her the right as an attorney to practice law in several courts within the state, and also stood as a testament as to why they could never have a serious, lasting relationship, no matter how much he thought about her, fantasized about her, wanted her. Those paper-thin parchments stood between them with the impenetrable strength of a solid concrete wall. One he'd never breach.

"You know, Jill," he began, circling the desk as she reached into the credenza for her purse. He might not care to breach the wall, but he had no qualms about climbing the fence for a better look. "There's one thing we haven't covered tonight."

"Hmm, what's that?" she asked, turning to face him.

He narrowed the small space between them. "What do we do about this?"

This was his hand slipping beneath the fall of her

hair to gently cup the back of her head as he slowly guided her toward his lips.

This had his heart pounding like a nervous teenager about to embark on his first kiss.

This was sweet anticipation firing up his desire.

"We haven't kissed yet." He gently brushed his lips over hers. "Engaged couples do kiss. A lot."

"They do more than kiss," she murmured, effectively hiking his temperature a few degrees. Her heavenly eyes held him spellbound, mesmerizing him with the heat and desire flaring to life in their welcoming depths, leaving no doubt in his mind that sex with Jill would be one of the most fascinating and sexually gratifying experiences of his adult life.

He wanted her. Bad. So bad he was starting to have doubts about getting involved with her. She represented everything he wanted in a woman, and the one thing he wouldn't, or couldn't, accept. Yet, he still wanted to taste her, still wanted to feel her slender body pressed against his, wanted her in the most intimate way a man could want a woman.

"So true." He placed gentle nips along her jaw. "And they touch," he whispered against her ear. "Touch me, Jill."

He grazed his teeth along the lobe of her ear, ignoring the clatter of her purse hitting the floor in favor of the feel of the slight tremble in her hands as she smoothed them over his chest. He sucked in a sharp breath as she wound them up over his shoulders to loop her arms around his neck, pressing her breasts against his chest.

She pulled back and looked up at him when his hands chased down her spine and settled on her lower back, holding her close. Her eyes, a deep shade of blue, filled with heat. His body responded instantly, hardening him in a flash. And he hadn't even kissed her yet!

"Just kiss me, Morgan." The first brush of her lips was tentative, the second, more bold. The third claimed him as hers.

Taking what she so willingly offered was easy, he thought as their tongues danced and chased.

Stopping was going to be another matter altogether.

5

THE RUSH OF EXCITEMENT, combined with a flash of heated desire, swept through Jill until her knees went weak. The blissful reality of Morgan's mouth drawing out her secrets and tasting her so sweetly, so...hungrily made her want with an intense need. She'd never been a prude, but the instantaneous ignition of sensuality shook her to the core.

With a soft moan, she wound her arms tighter around his neck, holding him close. She'd always believed there was a sensual creature lurking just below the surface, waiting to be tapped into and explored. He so effortlessly followed the trail, map in hands and flashlight beaming toward her hidden sensuality.

Her girlhood dreams of happily-ever-afters had matured into a reality filled with doubts of the existence of that all-too-elusive fairy-tale ending. She'd hoped there was just enough of that little girl left in her to believe that maybe, just maybe, someone special did exist just for her. That one special person who'd be able to reach the part of her protected from harm, deep down inside and perilously close to her heart. A place she'd sworn never to allow another man to tread.

Morgan couldn't be that man.

Or could he?

She'd done a lot of fantasizing about kissing him, and more, the past few days. Her imagination had conjured varying images, from sweet and tender to hot and erotic. Reality put her fantasies to shame.

She ached.

She needed.

She wanted him. Wanted him in the way a she-wolf seeks her mate. Wanted him in ways that should have shocked her, but instead made her feel brazen and surprisingly free.

Her fingers sifted through his black-as-midnight hair, and she aligned her body even closer to the length of his, reveling in the feel of his strength pressed against her. The soft, faded denim of his jeans brushed her legs. She wanted to feel the heat of his skin pressed intimately against her.

Oh sweet heaven, she wanted.

His hands chased up and down her spine. The warm, male scent of him wrapped around her. The feel of his tongue teasing hers in an ancient mating game fueled the sin-filled thoughts she'd embarked upon for the past ten days.

His mouth left hers to trail hot kisses along her jaw to that oh-so-sensitive spot on her throat. The man had built-in radar. He zeroed in on the exact place to touch with his tongue that made her tremble in his arms. She couldn't remember the last time a guy had made her tremble or feel so hot and restless.

"What are you doing to me?" he whispered, his breath hot against her ear.

"I could ask you the same question," she answered, turning her head to give him better access to her neck and throat. "You make me want things."

Her honest response should have had her stopping them before they went too far.

It didn't. On the contrary, she felt thrilled to the point of distraction.

"I want you, too, Jill. We should stop."

"Stop now and I'll have to hurt you," she said, placing biting little nips along his jaw. His answering chuckle rumbled through her.

She didn't want a man in her life. She didn't need a man to make her life complete. Yet, she couldn't shake the thought that Morgan could be the one man capable of finding that dark place in her soul and filling it with light.

Ludicrous.

How could she want Morgan? How could she want anyone? She didn't have time for a relationship.

She didn't want a relationship.

She didn't.

It's just sex.

That's it, she thought with a sense of profound relief. There was no deep-seated need *for* a mate, just *to* mate. Smoothing her hands over his shoulders and down his hard-as-granite torso, she knew what she wanted. Sex. A lot of it. A lot of it with Morgan.

Would he be willing to allow their relationship, such as it was, to become any more complicated? She wasn't asking for the fulfillment of emotional needs, just the quelling of the fierce sensual need rippling through her. She wasn't prepared for anything beyond a mutually gratifying sexual liaison. Sex she could handle. Anything deeper was out of the question. She'd gone that route once and would never allow anyone that close again. Just because she didn't want to end the deliciously wicked sensations coursing through her body didn't mean she was falling for Morgan. All it meant was that she was caught up in the magic of the sensual spell he'd cast over her, and in the instantaneous sparks of desire and need for fulfilment.

Sex.

Sex was the only kind of relationship they would ever share. Morgan was a caretaker. She didn't need to be taken care of—by anyone.

The hand smoothing down her back slid upward to cup her cheek, then gently eased into her hair to guide her mouth back to his. His palm was warm and slightly callused. His mouth was tender and seeking, making her feel as if she was the only woman in the world he wanted to kiss.

She reveled in the contradictory sensations, rough and tender at the same time.

His other hand fell to her hip, and he gently eased her away. Their bodies parted and she cursed the instant loss of heat and the overwhelming need to draw him back into her arms and kiss him senseless.

He looked down at her with that thundercloud-colored gaze. A gaze filled with sizzling heat that stroked her feminine pride. "We shouldn't do this," he rasped.

Oh, but she wanted to do *this*. Again and again until they reached that ultimate, and no doubt very satisfying, conclusion. If the man made love with one iota of the skill he kissed…

"You're right," she said, taking a step back. "This isn't the place."

He cleared his throat. "Jill, I don't think we should complicate things by becoming involved."

She frowned. Involved? An involvement was the last thing she was asking for—all she wanted was sex. Hot, sweaty-bodies sex that would leave them both exhausted and sated.

"I was thinking we could just have an affair."

His brows shot up and his eyes widened in shock.

A slow grin tugged her lips. "What? You think a preacher's daughter doesn't know a thing or two about sinning?"

He opened his mouth, then snapped it closed. He backed up a step and came in contact with her desk. He sat and stared at her.

"Morgan," she said, moving to stand in front him. "I'm not looking for a relationship. I have a career I'm trying to build, and relationships take way too much time and energy that I just don't have to give right now. What's wrong with just enjoying the next week together? We're both mature adults. We could have a fling."

"A fling?" His voice rose a notch. "You mean as in no attachments?"

She ignored the incredulity of his tone and smiled. "None whatsoever."

He shoved his hand through his hair and continued to stare at her as if she'd lost her mind. She hadn't. Not yet, but five days alone with him, with all that touching and kissing he'd claimed as common ground for engaged couples, she'd undoubtedly go insane.

"But what happens if..."

"Things get complicated?" She shook her head

adamantly. "Won't happen." She refused to let it happen. Complications were the reason she'd fabricated a fiancé. Complications were the reason she'd left Homer and moved to Los Angeles.

He crossed his arms over his chest and regarded her. Skepticism filled his gaze. "Anything is possible," he said, confusion evident in his rich, deep voice.

"We have nothing in common."

"Nothing except sex, is what you're saying."

She gave him her most wicked grin. "There is that," she said in a husky tone. She closed the small space between them and smoothed her hand down his chest. "And there could be a lot of that."

He placed his hand over hers when her fingers teased the flat nipple beneath his cotton shirt. "Jill, I don't know what to say."

She shrugged, hoping he'd think his answer was unimportant. "Don't say anything. If it happens, it happens. I want you, Morgan. I've never said that to another man. I don't want you to think I make a habit of this kind of thing. We're attracted to each other—"

"That much is obvious," he said dryly.

She grinned. "Then what's wrong with two people enjoying the pleasure of each other's bodies for a brief period of time?"

He stared at her in silence for a moment. Unable or unwilling to answer, she couldn't be sure. The only thing she was sure of was that for the first time in weeks, she was looking forward to the trip home for Carly's wedding with a new kind of excitement.

One that had very little to do with her little baby sister's upcoming nuptials.

A FLING. Jill wanted him. For sex. How was a guy supposed to respond to such a tempting request? he wondered, tossing the last of his shaving gear into the vinyl travel bag. It'd been days since her outrageous proposal, and he still hadn't decided if he was going to take her up on her very intriguing offer. He'd attempted to call her a few times, but they'd ended up playing phone tag. He'd eventually given up hope of actually speaking to her and finally left a message with her secretary telling her he'd meet her at the airport this morning.

"No parties," he said to his brother, walking back into the bedroom. "And no women allowed while I'm gone."

Will sighed and dropped onto the edge of Morgan's bed. "I know, I know. You've told me six times already."

"Just make sure you don't forget," Morgan said, giving Will a hard look. Who was he to lecture his kid brother? He was taking off for almost a week, lying to complete strangers and a mere heartbeat away from having an affair with a beautiful, sensual woman.

"You're just gonna have to trust me," Will said, taking a sip of the coffee he'd brought into the bedroom. "Besides, I'll probably be at work most of the time, anyway. There's a super sale on stereo equipment at the store this weekend, and I'm hoping to double my usual commission."

Morgan pulled the garment bag from the closet and laid it on the bed near his brother's feet. Will was a good kid, but having the house to himself could be just a little too tempting for a nineteen-year-old. Not for the first time, he'd wished Raina had come home for the summer so he wouldn't have to leave his brother alone.

"What do you need the extra money for?"

"I'd like to trade in that old beater for a model from this decade before I leave for school at the end of next month."

Morgan planted his hands on his hips. "Didn't I tell you I'd help you out with a new car? You don't have to work so hard, Will. You should be enjoying yourself."

Will grinned, his pale silver-blue eyes filling with laughter. "That's rich, coming from the Workaholics Anonymous poster child. When was the last time *you* took a vacation?"

"I'm taking one now, aren't I?" Morgan muttered. Since their mother had died six years ago he'd been working nonstop, first doing whatever he could to provide for the three of them, and finally, the past two years making Price Construction a small but successful drywall construction company. When Eleanor Price Blankenship had died, she'd done so without a will that would have provided for her youngest children. Regardless of how immoral, Ronald Blankenship had been within his legal right to take what had belonged to Eleanor and leave, with the exception of her minor children. Having nowhere or no one else to turn to, Morgan had assumed the responsibility of Will and Raina.

"Why are you such a grump?" Will asked after taking a swig of coffee. "For someone about to spend quality time with a hot number, you're sure in a mood this afternoon."

Morgan tossed his brother a disgruntled look.

"Who said she was a hot number?" If any of the guys—

"Sylvia told me. She said Jill was a real looker."

He'd have to remember to tell his secretary to keep out of his personal life. Not that he'd had one recently, but a guy did deserve some privacy.

"We won't be alone," Morgan said, pulling a couple of dress shirts and slacks from the closet. "We'll be staying at her parents' house. A house filled with out-of-town relatives."

"In-laws," Will teased with a mock shudder of revulsion.

Morgan frowned. "They're not my in-laws."

Will shrugged and set the mug on the bedside table. "Okay," he said, propping his hands behind his head. "Your future in-laws."

Morgan slipped his dress clothes into the garment bag. "They're *not* my future in-laws, either."

Will laughed. "Well, how about fake future in-laws? Tell me again why you're pretending to be some chick's fiancé?"

"Does temporary insanity count?" Morgan complained, zipping the garment bag closed. "And she's not some chick. She's..." a heavenly angel with a thoroughly sinful proposition. "Never mind."

There wasn't a man in his right mind who would turn down such a tempting offer. His mother, as absent as she'd been in their lives, *had* raised him to be a gentleman and to respect women. But what the hell was he supposed to do now that he'd been propositioned with a no-strings affair by a woman he couldn't stop thinking about for longer than six hours?

Comply? Just for the sake of sex? Even mind-blowing sex?

He might be an old-fashioned kind of guy, with old-fashioned values, but he wasn't a monk by any stretch of the imagination. He'd had his share of affairs over the years. Maybe there was something wrong with him, he wondered, crossing the bedroom to the dresser. Sex, just for the sake of sex, didn't appeal to him. Even when he was a teenager and supposedly plagued with raging testosterone levels, he'd had casual sex only a couple of times. Oh sure, he'd laugh and joke with the other guys in the locker room, and like most teenage boys, had been crude more times than he cared to recall, but he'd learned early on that he needed that all-important emotional attachment to a woman before embarking upon a physical relationship. Without the emotional, the physical was just...physical, and not anywhere near as satisfying.

He issued a few more orders to his brother while he finished packing, then loaded the bags in his truck. "The number where you can reach me is on the fridge."

Will stuffed his hands in the back pockets of his jeans. "I know, Morgan."

"And if you can't get hold of me," Morgan said, unlocking the truck door, "just call Sylvia."

Will sighed heavily, and shook a lock of dark hair off his forehead. "I know, Morgan."

Morgan frowned. "You sure you have enough money?"

"I've got plenty," Will said with a grin. "And I

promise to brush my teeth and floss before I go to bed every night."

Morgan chuckled. "Okay, I get the point."

Will clapped his hand on Morgan's shoulder. "Lighten up, big brother. And go have some fun for a change."

Morgan slid into the driver's seat and started the engine. With a final wave to his brother, he pulled out of the driveway and headed toward Los Angeles International Airport.

His brother wanted him to have fun. Maybe he *was* due for a little fun. He'd been the responsible one for such a long time, he didn't know if he had it in him to "lighten up."

Well, he thought as he merged onto the freeway, he could certainly try. Maybe a fling with a woman who turned him on with one sultry look or a beguiling, sweet smile was just what he needed to "lighten up." An affair with a woman who turned him inside out with need and desire. The same woman who could never become a permanent fixture in his life.

"YOU HAVE TO BE very careful what you say to my sister Alison. Whatever you tell her, you can't change your story. I swear, Ali can remember what she had for dinner six years, three months and twenty-two days ago."

Morgan glanced at Jill, who was busy fidgeting with the strap of her seat belt. "Relax," he said with a chuckle, shifting his attention back to the two-lane country highway. "It'll be fine."

"How can you say that?" she asked, her tone incredulous. "There's so much we didn't have a chance to go over that I just know something is going to go wrong somewhere."

He sighed. She was going to give herself an ulcer. "It's not because I wasn't available," he complained before he could stop himself. Okay, so he did feel a tiny stab of annoyance. Maybe if she hadn't arrived at the airport with a cellular phone glued to her ear, or spent three-quarters of the flight ignoring him in favor of typing away on her laptop and then sending the document by electronic mail to her secretary over the air-to-ground telephone, he wouldn't be feeling quite so resentful.

What bothered him even more, however, was that he cared. A dangerous state of mind for a guy intent on not getting involved with corporate-ladder types. His own childhood gave him more than enough reason. Couple that with the percentage of his employees with automatic payroll deductions to the courts for alimony and child support payments, and he had enough confirmation to cement his beliefs in stone.

She adjusted the visor to block the early evening sun. "That's not fair, Morgan. I already told you—"

"It's not important," he lied. It was damned important, but there wasn't a thing he could do about it, except maybe just enjoy the moment for a change. Something he'd been unable to do since his mother's bitterness had spurred her to embark upon a nasty custody battle where an impartial judge proclaimed Eleanor the winner, for the bargain price of her children's happiness.

He brought the rental sedan to a stop, glanced at the map and turned left toward the center of town. Homer, Illinois was quaint, and not unlike other small midwestern towns. As he drove down Main Street toward the parsonage, he had a hard time imagining the Jill he knew growing up in such a small, picturesque community.

"Take a left at the next corner," she instructed. "You sure sounded like it was important," she added in a tight voice.

He slung his arm over the wheel and glanced in her direction. "We shouldn't be arguing," he told her. "Your job is just as important to you as mine is to me."

She crossed her arms over her chest and gave him a level stare. "Exactly. So what's the problem?"

The problem was he liked her. And wanted her. From the second she'd walked into his life with her crazy ideas about the barter system, he'd been captivated by her. She'd been a constant in his mind from the moment he first set eyes on her when he'd gone to Nick for help. Jill Cassidy was everything a man could ever want in a woman, and everything *he* couldn't accept. The very traits he admired in her were the same ones that prevented him exchanging make-believe for reality. Make-believe was easier, he thought, turning left where she'd indicated. On Monday morning, they'd return to Los Angeles and their lives. Their *separate* lives.

"Morgan?" she prompted when he didn't immediately answer her.

He shot her another quick glance. "You really want to know?" At her nod, he said, "I like you, Jill. A lot. But it'd never work between us."

"Turn right, then left again and go to the end of the

block. I already told you I'm not looking for a relationship."

He made a right, followed by a quick left. "But what if I am?"

"You're kidding, right?" she asked. The anger he'd detected earlier in her voice faded, replaced by quiet surprise.

He supposed he was looking for the right woman. The right woman who would always put their family first. He pulled up to the curb of a Cape Cod style home with a neatly trimmed lawn shaded by large cottonwoods. He cut the engine before turning to face her. "I'm serious, Jill."

She stared at him, shock evident in her big blue eyes. "But? I hear a 'but' in that statement."

She claimed she wasn't looking for a relationship. If she'd been honest with him, then the truth wouldn't hurt her. "I wish you could be that woman, Jill, but you're not."

"Gee, thanks," she said, her tone dry. "You sure know how to sweet-talk a girl."

Despite the seriousness of their conversation, he laughed. "I didn't mean that like it sounded," he offered by way of an apology. "You're sweet, intelligent, and you excite the hell out of me, but you're already married—to your career."

"And you want a one...a one-track woman," she said after a moment, a hint of sadness in her voice. "What happened to you, Morgan?"

His standard answer died on his lips when he caught sight of the screened door to her parents' house swinging open, releasing a flood of males onto the lawn. "I thought you had six sisters?" he asked.

She glanced out the window. "Those are my brothers-in-law," she said, then turned back to face him, giving him a look that spoke loud and clear. They weren't finished with this conversation. Not by a long shot. He'd only been granted a brief stay.

From the determined look in his sinful angel's eyes, any pardon would be strenuously overruled.

6

JILL SAT perched on the wide arm of the overstuffed chair Morgan occupied, half listening to his conversation with her brothers-in-law Sean and Brad, a cabinetmaker and electrician respectively, about the ups and downs of the construction industry. Her father had yet to return, having gone to the train station in Chicago to pick up his ninety-five-year-old grandmother, who was coming in from Miami for the wedding. According to Ali's husband, Brad, more out-of-town relatives were due to arrive tomorrow.

She'd been granted a reprieve, albeit a slight one. She'd been dreading introducing Morgan to her father. She just knew he'd give her one of those looks that spoke louder than any sermon he gave on Sunday morning to his congregation. A look that said shame on her for keeping Morgan a secret for so long.

It was easy to keep a secret when the party in question had been a figment of her imagination. Now that the moment had arrived, she couldn't help but be relieved that she'd been so closemouthed about the man she'd created. At least there were fewer lies to trip them up during the week.

Her sisters, mother and both grandmothers had gone to her father's church to check on the non-floral decorations and would be returning soon, according to Marilee's husband, Sean. She was a bit disappointed that her sisters hadn't been there to greet them, but also slightly relieved. With only her and Morgan alone with all but one of the brothers-in-law, she had time to think about Morgan's less-than-flattering comment about her being the wrong woman.

Wrong woman, my Aunt Fannie.

Needing a few minutes alone, she excused herself and headed into the kitchen. A large oak table dominated the center of the spacious, sunlit room, the same table where she'd spent hours listening to her older sisters share stories about the opposite sex, where she'd battled the regimen of algebra and geometry, where she shared informal family meals and listened to her two grandmothers tell stories of growing up during the Depression and World War II.

The sound of children's laughter drew her attention, and she stepped over to the sink and peered out the window at her nieces and nephews playing in the backyard. The playhouse her father had built still stood in the corner of the yard. She smiled as the memory of the time she took a pair of child's scissors to Carly's hair drifted to her. Poor Carly, she thought with a smile. All those gorgeous long blond curls literally hacked away in uneven chunks.

Turning, she leaned against the Formica countertop and crossed her arms. Her gaze settled on the faded hot-pink stain she'd scrubbed and scrubbed for hours after spilling Brenda's nail polish. She'd been punished for taking something that didn't belong to her, and the stain had been a constant reminder to keep out of her oldest sister's room unless invited. A reminder she'd often ignored.

So many memories. Most of them happy, a few not so pleasant. Like when she told her father she was going away to law school. He'd been so proud of her for being accepted to University of California at Los Angeles's prestigious law school, but also disappointed she wouldn't be attending Northwestern, only a few hours away.

Or the day she'd informed her parents she was calling off the wedding to Owen and moving to California to take a job offer from the Public Defender's office.

And how could she forget when she'd sat at this very table and lied to her family the day they asked her if the rumor they'd heard about her engagement was true.

"You look sad."

She looked up at the sound of Morgan's husky voice and met his gaze. "Not sad. Just a little melancholy." She shrugged. "Coming home, I guess."

He moved to stand in front of her and gently settled his hands over her shoulders. "I like your family."

The sincerity in his eyes made her heart tighten in her chest. She didn't understand the emotion clogging her throat. Morgan was just playing a part, something she'd practically blackmailed him into doing for her. Why had he agreed? she wondered. Oh sure, he'd needed a lawyer for his foreman, something she'd capitalized on and taken advantage of to serve her own needs, but he could've hired any lawyer to get Eddie Burton off the hook. Could Morgan be lying to himself as much as she was?

She quickly set that disturbing thought aside. "The way my brothers-in-law have taken you in, I think the feeling's mutual. And they're only the tip of the iceberg," she told him wryly. "Beware. Before long there'll be a heck of a lot more of us Cassidys around than you'll know what to do with."

His hands gently rubbed her shoulders, then slid up to cup the back of her neck. "There's only one Cassidy I'm interested in at the moment."

She sighed. Yes. For the moment. Wasn't that what she'd told him in her office not too long ago? Let's have a fling and live for the moment no longer held the same appeal as it had when she'd first issued the offer of a no-strings affair.

She was having serious doubts in her ability to be a new-millennium kind of woman. Could there actually be just enough of those values her parents had instilled in her to keep her out of Morgan's bed?

She still wanted him—that hadn't changed. In fact, she wanted him with a need that demanded attention whenever he looked in her direction, or whenever he was close enough to touch. All she had to do was think about him and her temperature started to climb.

Maybe she could change his mind. First she'd have to find out what on earth had happened in his past. She couldn't very well fight a battle to win his heart when she had no clue about the enemy.

Nonsense, she thought. His heart was the last thing she wanted. He might be looking for forever, but happily-ever-after was *not* on her agenda. Just a mutually gratifying, and temporary, relationship.

She looked up at him and smiled, then slipped her arms around his neck. *Wrong woman, my Aunt Fannie.* He wanted her, and she was just the woman to prove it to him.

His hands eased from her neck and he clamped them on her arms at the elbow. When he didn't pull them from around his neck, she felt encouraged. When his dark eyebrows pulled together in a frown before he shot a glance over his shoulder to the doorway, she felt just a tad naughty.

"What are you doing?" he asked in a harsh whisper.

"We're engaged, remember?"

He looked at the doorway again, then back at her. "Someone might find us."

She smiled and inched closer until their bodies were perfectly aligned. At his sharp intake of breath when her breasts brushed against his chest, her smile widened. "That's the whole point, Morgan," she said patiently. "We're supposed to be in love. A stolen kiss or two is expected."

He stared down at her and groaned, fighting his own battle. His grip on her arms loosened and he skirted his hands down the length of her back.

"Just one kiss," she whispered, encouraged by his defeated groan.

"Just one," he said firmly, as if she was a little kid asking for an extra cookie before bedtime.

She wiggled closer and gently touched her mouth to his. "Only one," she said, before tracing her tongue along the seam of his lips.

His arms banded around her, holding her tight against him. "You play dirty, counselor," he said, then captured her lips in a hot, openmouthed kiss that had her knees weakening and her pulse clamoring.

Dizzying sensations traveled along her nerve endings at lightning speed. Heat balled in her tummy and spread outward, while need and desire ignited into an inferno of demand. The deep, tongue-tangling kiss left her feeling breathless, and with little doubt in her mind that it was her he wanted.

"Oh jeez, rent a room, will ya?"

Her first instinct was to ignore her older sister Lisa, but Morgan was already pulling away from her.

"Lisa. I...uh...didn't hear you come in," Jill said sheepishly, slipping her arms from around his neck.

Morgan stepped aside and Jill cast him a quick glance filled with apprehension before turning her attention back to the woman with a diaper bag slung over her shoulder, an infant carrier in her arms and a hint of laughter mingled with curiosity in her pale blue gaze. The family resemblance was obvious, but Jill was taller, her hair a lighter shade of blond.

Morgan wasn't comfortable perpetuating the lie that had been created to protect a fifty-year-old friendship, and to keep the matchmakers of Jill's family from parading every eligible bachelor in front of her. Having already met a few of the members of her family, what had seemed like a solution to both of their problems suddenly didn't feel right at all. He'd meant what he'd said when he'd told her he liked her family. Lying to them was wrong, but until Jill was prepared to put an end to the farce, his hands were tied. He wouldn't embarrass her, and a promise was a promise.

The woman set the infant carrier on the table and laughed. "Obviously." She crossed the room and gathered Jill in a welcoming hug. "We missed you, kid," she said, affection evident in her voice.

The door swung open and more women, all with that strong family resemblance, filed into the room. They were all attractive, but none of them had the same spun-gold hair as Jill, or the exact shade of her intriguing sapphire eyes.

And none of them were capable of sending need crashing through his body.

"The prodigal daughter returns," the leader of the pack called out in good humor.

"You're here!" another exclaimed when she caught sight of Jill.

Jill laughed. "You didn't really think I'd miss your wedding, did you?" she asked, gathering her baby sister in a hug.

Carly's grip on Jill loosened, and Morgan noted a hint of panic in her turquoise eyes.

"Not if you ever expected me to speak to you again," Carly teased. The slight quaver in her voice kept Morgan from believing all was well with Jill's youngest sister, and he wondered if Jill noticed. Prewedding jitters? Or something else?

"Ha, I should be so lucky," Jill said with a laugh, then hugged Carly again.

From the brief conversation they'd had on the plane, he knew she was close to all of her sisters, but Jill, Carly and Ali shared a special bond. They were the youngest three of the seven Cassidy daughters, and a six-year gap existed between Ali and Marilee, otherwise known as Chickie. She'd told him she'd heard her mother say on more than one occasion that having the girls so far apart was almost like having two families. The fact four years separated even Jill and Carly obviously made little difference to either of them.

Morgan remained by the counter, watching Jill with her sisters, listening to the feminine laughter and good-natured ribbing. Considering he'd practically raised his own sister, he wasn't too uncomfortable with all those women around, until a silence fell over the room and six pairs of varying shades of blue eyes locked on him.

Jill pulled in a deep breath and reached for his hand. The way her gaze caught his, he knew she was nervous, and he had to wonder if she wasn't feeling just a tad guilty. He gave her hand a gentle squeeze, hoping she'd draw comfort from the small gesture.

"Everybody," she said eventually, "this is Morgan."

The bride-to-be grinned. "Carly," she said by way of introduction.

One sister eyed him with caution. "Ali."

The one Jill had called Lisa waved a cloth diaper in his direction then laid it over her shoulder before lifting the baby in her arms.

The tallest of the Cassidy women crossed the kitchen toward him. "Welcome, Morgan," she said, extending her slender hand. "I'm Marilee, but everyone calls me Chickie."

"It's a pleasure," he said, taking her hand.

Wendy and Brenda introduced themselves. "There'll be a pop quiz later," Wendy teased.

"Wendy's a math teacher at the local high school," Jill explained, reaching for the baby in Lisa's arms. "Give me my niece."

"I'll do my best to study," he said to Wendy, unable to draw his gaze away from Jill cradling the infant in her arms. Something inside him squeezed. Was that his heart?

"Where's Mom?" Jill asked, settling into one of the chairs at the table.

Lisa spread the burp rag over Jill's shoulder and handed her the bottle she'd pulled from the diaper bag. "She and Grandma Lydia stopped at the market. Grandma Shirlee went home to rest before supper and to check on Granddad," Lisa explained. "Everyone is due back here at seven."

"Everyone?" Jill asked, keeping her attention on the baby in her arms.

"Everyone," Chickie said. "You wouldn't believe the family that's coming in tomorrow. Tonight will be peaceful in comparison to the rest of the week."

"This place will be bursting with relatives. It's like they're all coming to see the freak show at the circus," Carly complained, pulling out a chair from the table. "Even some of Dad's Wyoming cousins are coming for the wedding."

"You're the baby, Carly. It's expected," Ali explained with a grin that was short-lived. She cast her suspicious gaze Morgan's way. "Do you come from a large family, Morgan?"

"He has a younger brother and sister," Jill said before he could answer.

"What about your parents?" Ali asked, taking a seat between Jill and Carly at the table.

"They're gone now," he said.

"Ali, stop it," Jill warned.

"What? I'm only curious about the guy you say you're going to marry."

"You'll have to forgive Ali," Lisa said with a quick glance in Ali's direction. "Lately she's misplaced her share of the Cassidy humor gene."

Morgan wasn't sure if he was expected to laugh or not, so he took the safe route and kept a grin pasted on his face.

Ali rolled her eyes and stood. "Welcome to the family, Morgan," she said in a much more congenial tone. "I hope you can handle it."

"What gives?" Jill asked once Ali left the room.

"Don't ask me." Brenda slid a bowl of fresh fruit closer and helped herself to an apple. "She's been moody the past couple of weeks."

"What does Ali have to be moody about?" Wendy said, crossing the kitchen to the refrigerator. "That apartment she and Brad have across town isn't filling up with relatives."

"Our house will be bursting soon, too," Chickie added, "so stop complaining. We're all doing our share."

"I didn't want a big wedding," Carly grumbled.

"Stop sniveling, Carly," Jill chided her sister. "It's unbecoming for the bride to be so whiny."

"That's right," Wendy chimed in, pulling out a pitcher of lemonade followed by a bucket of ice from the freezer. "You're supposed to be glowing."

Morgan took the glass Wendy offered. He consid-

ered excusing himself from the group of women in favor of the baseball game the husbands had turned on
in the den, until Chickie ordered him to sit.

Let the interrogation begin, he thought as he com-
plied and sat across from Jill, whose attention was on
the baby she was crooning to in her arms. Funny, but
he'd never imagined her the type to be comfortable
around children. Legal briefs and courtrooms, yes.
Especially after she'd told him she refused to trade in
her briefcase for a diaper bag.

"How long have you two known each other?"
Chickie asked.

"Jill hasn't told us a thing about you," Brenda explained, giving the sister in question a narrowed
look.

"Have you set a date?" Carly asked.

"You will get married here, right?" Lisa wanted to
know.

"Of course they will," Wendy added. "What do
you do for a living, Morgan?"

"Oh please," Jill said, setting the empty bottle on
the table. She shifted the infant to her shoulder and
began a series of gentle, rhythmic pats on her back.
"You forgot the rubber hose and bright lights."

Chickie laughed. "Now why didn't I think of that
sooner? Where'd Dad leave his tool box?"

"It's okay," he said to Jill with a chuckle. "I have a
sister, remember?"

He leaned back in the chair and looked at Carly,
thinking of the best way to answer without actually
lying. "No date has been set yet," he answered, neither admission nor denial.

Shifting his attention to Lisa, he said, "There's been

no discussion of where the wedding will take place, but I'm sure Jill will want to get married here."

"I'm a drywall contractor," he told Wendy. "I have a small company in Riverside, where I live."

Finally, turning his attention to Brenda, he asked, "Any questions?"

She grinned. "Only one. How did my prodigal sister find you?"

"You don't want to know," he said with an answering grin.

"Ooh, I do," Chickie said, rising from the table. "But it'll have to wait. We have five kids in the backyard that are going to need to be bathed before supper, and it's getting late."

"You want me to take her?" Lisa asked Jill.

Jill shook her head. "Go take care of the little ones. Francesca and I are doing just fine. Aren't we, sweetie-pie?" she crooned to the infant nestled against her.

Carly excused herself, as did Wendy and Brenda, leaving Jill and Morgan alone.

He braced his arms on the table and looked at Jill as the room cleared. Her gratitude-filled gaze met his. "You were perfect. Thank you."

"It wasn't any less than I expected," he said. What he hadn't expected was how much he liked her sisters. From the way Jill had talked about her family, he hadn't expected such a fun-loving bunch, quick to smile and equally quick to tease, especially with a fire-and-brimstone preacher as the family patriarch. She claimed she was nothing like her sisters. In his opinion, she had more in common with them than she believed.

"Are you sure we're staying here?" he asked her. "Your sister said the house was already full."

She bit her lip. "Yes, but surely..."

He gave her a lopsided grin and stood. "You didn't check, did you?"

She looked up at him and shook her head. "I just assumed we'd be staying here. Morgan, what are we going to do?"

He crouched beside her, lightly smoothing his hand over the sleeping infant's back. "Is there a motel in town?"

Her eyes brightened with hope. "Good idea," she said, and thrust the sleeping baby into his arms. "I'll call ahead."

Before he could protest, she left him alone in the kitchen. He looked down at Francesca, completely oblivious to the stranger holding her. For the second time that day he found himself with a female in arms that he had no clue what do with—except hold close, next to his heart.

7

JILL STOOD in the doorway of her new home away from home, her gaze locked on the queen-size bed. On the single, queen-size bed.

"I can't believe this is happening," she groaned, then stepped reluctantly into the quaintly furnished room of the Village Inn.

Morgan set their bags near the mirrored double doors of the closet and looked around. "Nice room," he said, then crossed the plush navy carpeting to the double French doors.

Room. As in singular. Not *rooms,* plural, as she'd requested. Only one room and only *one* bed.

Oh good grief, what was she going to say to her family? No doubt word had already spread that the preacher's daughter was shacking up with some guy, thanks to Mabel Chancellor, town gossip and proprietor of the only accommodations within a thirty-mile radius of Homer.

"Have you seen this?" Morgan asked, pushing open the French doors. "We have our own private terrace."

She sat on the floral tapestry chair and dropped her head into her hands. It didn't matter that she and Morgan were supposedly engaged to be married. The preacher's daughter did not share a room, even temporarily, with a man to whom she was not legally wed, and especially one she had no intention of marrying, regardless of what her family and the town of Homer believed.

"I'm sorry, Jill," Mabel Chancellor had said with a shake of her salt-and-pepper hair. "With Carly's wedding, we're booked solid."

She'd been a breath away from turning down the room when Morgan had laid his credit card on the counter. "We'll take it. We don't have a choice," he'd told her.

The Village Inn was a small lodge, with only a half dozen cottages to its name. Considering the size of her family and the relatives coming in from out of town for the grand occasion, it was easy to believe the small establishment was booked solid.

"What's the matter?" Morgan asked from the open doorway of the terrace. A backdrop of white-and-pink climbing roses along with a soda fountain table and two chairs filled the small terrace. A more romantic setting she couldn't have created.

"My father is going to kill me," she said, dread tightening her throat. She slid down in the chair and stared up at the ceiling. "I didn't even *think* about accommodations," she complained. "I always stay at my parents' house."

The parsonage wasn't overly large and only boasted four bedrooms. Growing up, Brenda as the eldest, had her own room. Lisa, Marilee and Wendy had shared a room, leaving her, Carly and Ali to bunk together. Brenda's room had become her mother's sewing room and doubled as a guest room, which would be occupied by her great-grandmother.

Grandma Lydia had moved into Lisa, Marilee and Wendy's old room shortly after her husband had passed away. That left the fold-out sofa in the den, which Lisa, her husband, Ron, and baby Francesca had claimed for the week, with Ron, Jr. and little Emily sharing the bride-to-be's bedroom. More out-of-town aunts, uncles and cousins were already staying with Chickie, Wendy and Brenda, with others due at the Village Inn over the next two days. They were lucky to even get a room, according to Mabel.

The Cassidy Clan had definitely returned to Homer.

Morgan re-entered the room and sat on the edge of the *only* bed. Bracing his arms on his knees, he looked over at her, a hint of mischief in his eyes.

"We are engaged," he told her, humor lacing his tone.

She gave him a look that said she didn't find him, or his ill-timed humor, amusing.

Amusing? No.

Sexier than any man she'd ever encountered?

Oh yeah.

"I don't recall a clause in our rules of engagement about sharing a hotel room," she said eventually.

He reached over and settled his hand on her denim-clad knee. "Jill, we're not doing anything wrong."

Ha! That's what he thought. She could quote him chapter and verse about the sins of impure thoughts, of which she'd had plenty. Considering where her mind had taken up residence, she was destined for a front-row seat somewhere where snowballs didn't stand a chance of survival.

"We didn't have any other choice," he added, giving her knee a gentle squeeze. She attempted to ignore the sparks shooting up her leg and settling in her tummy, and failed.

She pulled in a deep breath and let it out slowly. So what if everyone knew she and Morgan were staying at the inn together? she thought rebelliously, and sat up straighter. Big deal. They were both adults. Adults everyone believed engaged to be married. Homer may be a throwback to *Mayberry R.F.D.*, but Jill Cassidy had stepped right off of Wilshire Boulevard, where sharing a hotel room with a man was as common as rush-hour traffic.

"Besides," Morgan said, drawing her attention to the lopsided grin tipping his oh-so-sexy mouth, "nothing is going to happen."

Now there was a point she could easily argue. Morgan's objection was a mountain she had every intention of climbing, and conquering. She grinned. "Really? We will be sleeping in the same bed, you know."

His grin faded. "Sleeping, Jill. That's all we'll be doing."

"Hmm." She stood and grabbed her suitcase, ignoring the firmness of his voice. Setting it on the bed beside Morgan, she snapped the locks and flipped it open.

"What does that mean?" he asked.

"Nothing," she said with an innocence she was suddenly far from feeling. Morgan was a challenge. Too bad he didn't know she thrived when challenged.

Poor man. He was about to embark upon a path of discovery he'd never forget.

Lifting the sheer cream teddy she'd bought with him specifically in mind, she felt decidedly wicked. Rising to the challenge, she turned to face him, holding the whisper-thin material against her. The look filling his gaze told her his thoughts were equally wicked.

"It just sounds like you're trying to convince yourself that's all we'll be doing," she said, then refolded the teddy to place in the drawer of the dresser.

He let out a long breath of air and stood. "Maybe I am," he admitted, looking down at her.

She pulled a satin floral chemise from her suitcase. Desire flashed in his eyes.

Oh yeah, they would definitely be dancing the horizontal mambo before heading back to their separate lives. An experience she had no doubt would be more than pleasurable. She only hoped that in conquering his objections, she didn't lose sight of her own important goals.

"Don't you own any flannel?" he groused.

She gazed up at him with feigned innocence, slowly shaking her head. "I like the feel of satin against my body."

She held the nightie toward him, the thin spaghetti straps looped loosely over her fingers. He backed up a step as if she held something cold-blooded and poisonous. She suspected the nightie was stirring some very interesting thoughts in his mind.

At least she hoped so. Hers was working overtime.

"Go ahead," she coaxed, dropping her voice to a

husky purr reserved for moonlit nights. "Touch it. Feel the way it just glides across your skin."

He tucked his fingers in the front pockets of his jeans.

Disappointed, but far from discouraged, she shrugged and gently folded the nightie, then turned to place it in the drawer with the teddy.

"What are you doing?" he asked when she pulled a stack of lacy panties and matching bras from her suitcase. She hadn't really imagined the slight panic in his voice, had she?

She glanced over her shoulder, then quickly turned away to hide the smile on her lips. Most definitely panic.

"Unpacking." She added a few camisoles to the drawer. "We're supposed to be at my parents' house in a little over an hour for dinner. I'd like to shower and change, but I need to unpack first."

He muttered something about water temperature she didn't quite catch, then snagged his bag and disappeared into the bathroom.

She let out a sigh and continued unpacking. She didn't feel much like a conquering warrior, but at least she'd managed to draw her opponent into the open...until he'd retreated to the bathroom. She wasn't discouraged. By the time she finished with her suitcase, she still had hope of emerging victorious.

Too bad her faith in happily-ever-after had become so tarnished, she thought, hanging her garment bag and Morgan's in the closet. His noble intentions were commendable, and no matter how endearing, unnecessary. He was the kind of guy who could easily restore her faith in fairy tales, if she let herself be swept away by all that nobility and honor. The fact that he had knight-in-shining-armor written all over his glorious body didn't hurt, either.

And she'd always been a voracious reader.

MORGAN HAD BEEN fairly certain of what to expect as far as Jill's parents were concerned. From their conversations, she'd claimed her mother was a combination of Donna Reed and June Cleaver. Her father was supposedly a stern, lecturing pastor, more condemning than concerned, more judgmental than loving.

He'd been misled on both counts.

His first doubts had surfaced after meeting Jill's sisters. Those easy smiles had to come from somewhere. Quick grins and sharp wit couldn't have been second nature to the Cassidy women if they hadn't been surrounded by that kind of love and humor. The way Jill had spoken of her father, he'd suspected those qualities were solely the product of Jill's mother, Marilyn, but meeting Reverend Richard Cassidy told an entirely different story.

Sparkling blue eyes that looked upon his family with deep affection, along with a ready smile and plenty of laughter, embodied the good reverend. Marilyn was just as warm and loving.

Feminine laughter drifted through the open kitchen windows as Jill and her sisters cleaned up after the huge family dinner. At dinner, he'd met the rest of the husbands, along with Jill's grandparents and great-grandmother. Love and laughter had been served up with a meal like nothing he'd ever experienced. Two tables had been set in the spacious formal dining room to accommodate the large crowd, and he couldn't help being awestruck by the efficiency and calm with which Mrs. Cassidy had managed to serve a delicious meal for so many people. His own mother couldn't have been bothered to prepare a meal for four.

A deep longing he'd thought buried resurfaced. Not once since his parents' divorce could he recall a scene like the one he'd been a part of tonight. Happy family dinners were non-existent after he, Raina and Will had been moved to California. In fact, he couldn't really remember many happy moments before the divorce, now that he thought about it. Once his mother had opted for a career, family dinners were only one of the traditions that had become virtually extinct in the Price household. His father had tried for a time, but even Kenneth Price had grown tired of attempting to keep up the pretense of the happy family.

This was what he wanted, Morgan thought, bracing his hands behind him on the back-porch railing. He wanted his family to be happy, to share laughter and lots of love, and even tears. The only way he knew of to accomplish that for the children he hoped to have some day was to marry the right woman. A woman whose primary focus would be her family and not a climb up the corporate ladder. He'd seen far too many marriages crumble because of ambition to accept anything less.

"He's the strong, silent type," Jill's mother said in a bad stage whisper to the reverend, who was sitting beside her on the porch swing.

"Probably because Jilly doesn't give him a chance to speak," Jill's grandfather added, tapping his pipe in the palm of his hand. "Never could keep that girl quiet for more than five minutes."

Morgan grinned but remained silent when a movement through the kitchen window caught his attention. The woman in question stood on a step stool with a crystal bowl in her hand as she stretched to place it on the top shelf. The hem of her red silk blouse inched up over the band of her black slacks, giving him a peek at lightly tanned skin.

The woman was bad for his rapidly slipping self-control.

His convictions were being tested by a sexy temptress with sin on her mind.

A test he was a heartbeat away from flunking.

Jill turned and laughed, her eyes dancing with the same mischief she'd baited him with at the inn. She grabbed the dish towel draped over her shoulder and tossed it at Carly. A sense of loneliness he hadn't felt since his mother had moved her children from the only home they'd ever known washed over him. This was what he wanted, but not with Jill. She was the wrong woman for him no matter how much she excited him or how close he was to falling for her delectable charms. What he wanted with Jill was physical. He couldn't deny the truth...or the cold shower he'd taken when she'd heated his blood close to boiling by striking a match to his imagination. Having an affair with her could be nothing more than short-term.

No, what he longed for was the kind of open and harmonious relationship Jill's family shared. He wanted the laughter, something that had been missing from his life for too long. He wanted the closeness, something he'd assumed he shared with Raina and Will until he saw Jill's family and the way they laughed, talked and teased, the way they supported each other without an ounce of judgment. Jill may be the only Cassidy to have flown far from the nest, but that didn't mean her family was any less proud of her for her accomplishments. They simply wanted her close, not because they wanted to control her life, but because they cared.

The longing sweeping through him intensified. He didn't want love and support cloaked in obligation. Just love. With the *right* woman.

Jill knew how to give all those things, he thought as he continued to watch, smiling when she laughed at something Brenda said. She gave without thought or effort. Those qualities were just *there*, a part of who she was, something she'd no doubt pass along to her children in the same unconscious manner the reverend and Mrs. Cassidy had to their daughters.

Too bad she was the wrong woman.

Richard Cassidy stood and looked pointedly at Morgan. "Have you had a chance to see Marilyn's prized roses, son?"

"No sir, I haven't," he answered, knowing he about to be invited to observe flowers neither one of them had any interest in viewing.

"Then you're in for a treat," Richard said, clapping his hand over Morgan's shoulder. "They're especially lovely under the light of a full moon."

"Honestly, Richard. Do you think you could be just a little more transparent? I don't think Morgan realizes you're about to give him one of those 'you're marrying my daughter' lectures," Ethel Cassidy, Jill's great-grandmother said, shaking her head in mock disgust.

To her granddaughter-in-law she said, "I'd hoped after forty years of marriage you'd have taught him some diplomacy, Marilyn."

"I've tried, Gran," she answered, patting the older woman's hand affectionately. "Believe me, I have tried."

Richard laughed and stepped off the porch. "I'm sure Morgan isn't surprised that I'd like a word alone with my future son-in-law. Jilly no doubt warned him."

"It's not so bad," Sean, Chickie's husband, teased as Morgan walked down the brick steps to the backyard to join Jill's father.

"Consider yourself lucky, Morgan," Paul, Brenda's husband, called after them. "Hey, Dean. Didn't you say he's mellowed with age?"

Carly's future husband chuckled. "He didn't pull out the .22, if that's what you mean by mellow."

Richard waved his hand in affectionate dismissal at his sons-in-law before ushering Morgan along the brick path toward the side of the house.

The evening was pleasant, with a slight breeze coming from the south filling the warm night air with the scent of pine and roses. Despite the serenity, guilt plagued Morgan. The thought of lying to Richard bothered him. Not just because her father was a man of the cloth, but because he liked these people. They were open and honest, and they'd welcomed him into their home and into their family without question.

They walked in companionable silence to the front

of the house. Richard climbed a couple of steps and sat, then waited quietly for Morgan to do the same.

"Do you come from a large family, Morgan?" the reverend asked, looking up at the star-filled sky. "My daughter has been remarkably silent about the man she intends to marry."

"I have a younger brother and sister," he answered, adding the standard statistical information, grateful he hadn't been put in a position of dishonesty. Yet.

"And your parents?" he asked, shifting his piercing blue eyes to Morgan.

Morgan leaned forward, bracing his elbows on his legs, his hands clasped between his knees. "My parents divorced when I was a kid. They're both deceased now. I have a stepfather, but we're not really in touch."

"I'm sorry," the reverend said, his voice filled with compassion. "My father passed away recently, so I do know how you feel. It's never easy, and something you never really get over, do you?"

"No, sir," Morgan answered because it was expected. Although he'd made his peace a long time ago, there were occasions when he missed his old man, but because of the bitterness of the divorce, visits with his father were minimal. As for his mother, how could he miss someone who'd never really played an active role in his life? She provided for her children, but that had been the extent of Eleanor's maternal instincts. Her children hadn't wanted for anything, except her love and attention. And all Ronald Blankenship cared about was himself.

Richard looked at him, curiosity and something

else Morgan couldn't quite identify lingering in the older man's gaze. "I don't even know how you and my daughter met."

Morgan opted for a blemished version of the truth. "One of my employees needed a lawyer. Jill was it," he said with a shrug, carefully avoiding the exact terms of their retainer agreement.

"All my daughters are special, Morgan," Richard said. "But Jilly's different. I suppose you know that already."

Morgan couldn't argue. She was a sexy, tempting angel prepared to lead him down a path of unforgettable sin. He should've packed his hiking boots.

"My daughters, like my wife, are all independent. Jilly's definitely the most headstrong," he added with a warm chuckle. "It'll take a strong man to tame her."

Morgan issued a dry laugh. "I can't see anyone 'taming' Jill," he stated honestly. The idea was ridiculous. Jill was a woman who knew what she wanted and went after it with a damn-the-torpedoes mentality he reluctantly admired. The fact that she wanted him should have had him on the first flight back to L.A.

A neutron bomb couldn't have moved him off the porch.

Richard settled his hand on Morgan's shoulder. "That's good to hear, son," he said, relief evident in his voice and in his kind blue eyes. "Very good to hear."

Morgan frowned. "Excuse me?"

"She did tell you about Owen, didn't she?" her father asked carefully.

Morgan nodded. "I know they were engaged to be

married." She hadn't said much more than that and had only told him about Owen because he'd asked her specifically about ex-boyfriends.

"Then you understand my meaning," Richard said quietly.

No, he didn't, but nodded anyway. Asking Jill's father to enlighten him wasn't appropriate, either. Jill owed him the explanation.

He shook that thought from his mind. Jill owed him nothing, and if she'd been hurt in the past, it wasn't any of his business. They weren't involved, their liaison was merely temporary. Whatever happened to her was of no consequence to him.

So why did he feel like demanding she tell him everything about her former fiancé?

Because he cared about her.

He cared about her—a lot.

Of course he cared about her. Just the way he cared about a lot of people. His brother and sister, his secretary, Sylvia, and every one of his employees. If he didn't care, he wouldn't be sitting on the front porch with the good reverend now.

Yet he couldn't deny the truth. No one else caused his gut to twist with need the way Jill did, or his heart to lurch painfully in his chest at the thought of her being hurt. Nor could he deny the emotion rearing its ugly head at the mention of Jill's former fiancé as anything but jealousy.

8

MORGAN UNLOCKED the door to the small cottage, then held it open for Jill to pass. He caught a whiff of her perfume, the scent wrapping around him and luring him in with seductive magic. His tried-and-true argument about her not being the right woman was getting old. She might not be the one he planned to spend the rest of his life with, but there was a connection between them he was finding more and more difficult to deny.

She dropped her purse on the dresser, then turned to face him. "You've been silent long enough," she said, worry banked in her gaze. "What did you and my father talk about?"

He let out a sigh, then moved to the tapestry chair and sat. "You," he said, bracing his elbows on his knees.

She planted her hands on her hips and gave him a level stare. "I figured that much," she said with more than a hint of sarcasm. "Details, Morgan. I want details."

So did he. Such as, what really happened between her and Owen Kramer that had Reverend Cassidy concerned about him "taming" Jill?

"Our little secret is safe, if that's what you're worried about," he told her. For how long, he didn't want to estimate. Lying to her father wasn't something he wanted to do. He not only liked Reverend Cassidy, he respected him. Repaying that respect with dishonesty wasn't right.

The frown tugging her brows together smoothed. She pushed off the dresser and moved to the bed. "Was he just curious about you? Or did he give you the speech he's given to all my brothers-in-law?"

"The...what did your great-grandmother call it? Oh yeah, the 'you're marrying my daughter' speech?"

She eased onto the foot of the bed and lay on her side facing him, using her elbow for support. Her mouth tipped into a beguiling smile, drawing his gaze to her lips. Lord, he wanted to kiss her.

Her hand settled over the gentle slope of her hip, coming to rest on her thigh. "That would be the one."

"Background mostly." He followed the movement of her hand with his eyes, resisting the urge to follow with his own hands, to smooth them over her slender curves and make her his. "He also seemed relieved that I knew about your engagement to Owen," he said, dragging his eyes back to her face, and stalling for far too long at her lips. "Now why would that be?"

Anger momentarily flared in the depth of her gaze, followed by a flash of pain he felt clear to his heart. "Owen Kramer is a nonissue."

Morgan stared at her, surprised by the hardness in her voice. Her reaction said Kramer *was* still an issue.

She shot off the bed, then flung open the French doors. "It's stuffy in here," she said in a softer tone before stepping onto the semiprivate terrace.

The Harlequin Reader Service® — Here's how it works:

Accepting your 2 free books and gift places you under no obligation to buy anything. You may keep the books and gift and return the shipping statement marked "cancel." If you do not cancel, about a month later we'll send you 4 additional novels and bill you just $3.34 each in the U.S., or $3.80 each in Canada, plus 25¢ shipping & handling per book and applicable taxes if any.* That's the complete price and — compared to cover prices of $3.99 each in the U.S. and $4.50 each in Canada — it's quite a bargain! You may cancel at any time, but if you choose to continue, every month we'll send you 4 more books, which you may either purchase at the discount price or return to us and cancel your subscription.

*Terms and prices subject to change without notice. Sales tax applicable in N.Y. Canadian residents will be charged applicable provincial taxes and GST

If offer card is missing write to: Harlequin Reader Service, 3010 Walden Ave., P.O. Box 1867, Buffalo NY 14240-1867

NO POSTAGE
NECESSARY
IF MAILED
IN THE
UNITED STATES

BUSINESS REPLY MAIL
FIRST-CLASS MAIL   PERMIT NO. 717   BUFFALO, NY

POSTAGE WILL BE PAID BY ADDRESSEE

HARLEQUIN READER SERVICE
3010 WALDEN AVE
PO BOX 1867
BUFFALO NY 14240-9952

GET FREE BOOKS and a FREE GIFT WHEN YOU PLAY THE...

Lucky 7

SLOT MACHINE GAME!

Just scratch off the silver box with a coin. Then check below to see the gifts you get!

YES! I have scratched off the silver box. Please send me the 2 free books and gift for which I qualify. I understand I am under no obligation to purchase any books, as explained on the back of this card.

342 HDL C4GM

142 HDL C4GD
(H-T-OS-08/00)

| | | | | | | | | | | | | | | |

NAME   (PLEASE PRINT CLEARLY)

| | | | | | | | | | | | | | | |

ADDRESS

| | | | | | | | | | | | | | | |

APT.#   CITY

| | | | | | | | | | | | | |

STATE/PROV.   ZIP/POSTAL CODE

7 7 7 Worth **TWO FREE BOOKS** plus a **BONUS** Mystery Gift!

Worth **TWO FREE BOOKS!**

Worth **ONE FREE BOOK!**

TRY AGAIN!

DETACH AND MAIL CARD TODAY!

Common sense told him to leave it alone. His curiosity wouldn't let him, so he followed her outside. She stood facing the rose-covered lattice, tracing the delicate petal of a soft pink bloom with her fingertips. "I make one error in judgment and everyone thinks..." She sighed and turned to face him. "Owen Kramer was a mistake. One I don't ever plan on repeating."

His imagination kicked into overdrive, conjuring all sorts of scenarios, none of them happy. "What happened?"

She shrugged, then turned her attention back to the flowers. "He wasn't *the one.*"

No, he didn't imagine Kramer had been, but that still didn't answer his question. Or tell him about the pain he'd seen in her eyes. "Did he hurt you?" he prompted.

She took so long in answering, he started to worry. If the SOB had laid a hand on her, so help him...

"Not the way you're thinking," she finally said, as if she'd read his mind. "We just had different ideals. He wanted a wife completely devoted to him and wasn't willing to share her with a career."

Something he completely understood, but even he wasn't that selfish. The devotion he expected wasn't for him, but for the family he hoped to have some day. If the future Mrs. Price wanted to work outside the home, fine, so long as her family was always her first priority. He wasn't exactly looking for a stay-at-home, cookie-baking, PTA-involved kind of woman, just one who would put her family above all else. He'd be damned if his children would suffer the way he had.

"Is that why you called it off?" he asked, shoving his hands into his trouser pockets.

"Something like that." She glanced over her shoulder at him. "Do we really have to talk about this now?"

There was something in her voice, a quality he couldn't quite put his finger on, telling him she was avoiding an important issue.

Something that could make a difference?

To him?

To them?

He should have let the subject drop. He should have turned and walked back into their room, flipped on the television and settled down to watch *The Tonight Show* and forget about Jill and her disastrous near marriage to the wrong guy.

He couldn't. For the life of him, he couldn't leave the subject alone any more than he could stop the unavoidable. He cared about Jill. He wanted her. All that stood between them was the same old issue, and he was tired of thinking about it. She'd never give up her career, and he'd never ask her to give up something she'd worked hard to attain.

Making love to her was as inevitable as the sun rising. Standing behind her on the terrace, he was hit full force with the acknowledgment. They would make love, that all-important emotional attachment included in the bargain. He refused to label it as love, and forever just wasn't an option. All they had was the moment. The very idea transcended common sense, but he couldn't deny he cared about Jill more than was wise, and more than he'd ever intended.

Cautiously, he eased his arms around her waist

and pulled her against him. He didn't expect her to push him away. No, the caution in his actions stemmed from his own wariness combined with a fear that could lead him straight into heartache if he wasn't very careful.

Her back flush against his chest, she rested her head against his shoulder. Smoothing her hands over his arms, she sighed. "Hmm. This is nice."

He thought so, too, breathing in the alluring fragrance of her perfume mingled with the delicate scent of roses. They might be all wrong for each other, but her body pressed against his felt too right to be anything but pure perfection.

"Tonight's conversation with your dad was just the tip of the iceberg," he said quietly, resting his chin atop her head. "He's going to ask more questions, and I need to know the right answers. He's worried about you, Jill, afraid that you're going to repeat whatever mistake you made before."

Silence. A deafening silence that lent credence to his suspicions of a pain-filled past.

He waited patiently, simply holding her against him, waited for her to tell him the truth.

"I've known Owen since the third grade," she explained, trailing her fingertips absently along his forearms in light, gentle strokes. "Our parents were close friends, and Owen had always just been there as a part of my life. My last year of college, we started dating, but it didn't get serious until my second year of law school. Even then we only saw each other on breaks.

"Have you ever thought you had everything where you wanted it, and then—*wham*—something comes along and changes all of your plans? That's what happened to me when Owen proposed. My last year of law school, I started interviewing in L.A. The Public Defender's office offered me a sweet deal starting in the fall. I accepted, knowing once I passed the bar I'd gain more trial experience there than in a large firm, but then I came home, and Owen proposed."

He detected a hint of bitterness in her voice and could sympathize with her. His situation had been different, but he'd exchanged his future plans for the care and well-being of Raina and Will. Regret hadn't been an option. He'd done what he'd had to do, and would do it again without question.

"We'd planned to marry in the early fall," she said. "Owen wouldn't even consider moving to California, so the job wasn't going to happen for me. I accepted that, but was still disappointed. I thought I was in love and everything was going to be wonderful. We'd have this great life. He's an investment broker and I'm a lawyer. We'd make oodles of money, have a fabulous house in Lake Forest, two point five kids and a golden retriever named Annie."

"But it didn't happen," he said, tightening his hold.

She sighed and shook her head. "No. And I'm really glad it didn't. We were so wrong for each other.

"Hindsight and all that, I guess I had my doubts at the time because I never told anyone about the job offer in L.A. Both of our parents were thrilled with our engagement, and my mom and Owen's practically took over the wedding plans.

"So, I let them pretty much plan my wedding while I studied for the bar exam and started interviewing with firms in Chicago. I had a couple of really great offers with two prestigious firms. Owen worked in Chicago, so as the wedding got closer, I mentioned we should start looking at apartments in the city. That was when I found out he planned to live right here in Homer."

She turned in his arms and looked up at him. A slight frown marred her forehead, and a heated remnant of resentment filled those expressive eyes. The urge to kiss away that frown and fill her gaze with another kind of heat overwhelmed him.

"You start factoring in rush-hour traffic," she said, "and you're looking at a little over four hours on the road. As a new associate in a big firm, I'd be facing twelve-hour days or longer, so I told him I had no intention of living in Homer. I'd be willing to compromise and find a place in the suburbs since he didn't want to live in the city, but he refused. When I asked him how I was supposed to get back and forth to work, especially in the winter, that was when he told me that no wife of his would be working for a living, so I was just wasting my time interviewing."

"That's way too unreasonable," he heard himself saying despite his convictions. "You spent—what— over seven years of your life studying to become a lawyer?"

She slipped out of his embrace. "It's all I ever wanted. When other kids were watching *Bugs Bunny*, I was channel surfing for reruns of *Perry Mason* or trying to find ways to convince my dad to let me stay up late on Thursday nights to watch *L.A. Law*. Owen knew that about me."

"And you'd had no idea how he felt?" He'd made his own position perfectly clear and had a hard time imagining being that close to a woman and her not having an inkling of his feelings on certain issues.

"Then I didn't," she said, propping her backside against the soda fountain table. "Looking back, I can see I just wasn't paying attention. There were little things I chose to ignore."

He crossed his arms over his chest. "Such as?"

"Aside from a general lack of enthusiasm?" At his nod, she said, "Double-edged comments, mostly. He's a textbook case of a passive-aggressive personality at its best."

"Or its worst, depending on how you look at it."

Her mouth tipped into a wry grin. "True. But there were other things, too," she said. "I refused to give up something I'd worked so hard for, but at least *I* was willing to compromise. He was just as adamant about living in town, so I stopped fighting with him about it and met with our state's attorney for the county. Carl Atkinson agreed to take me on as a part-time law clerk until I passed the bar. Once I had my license, I planned to register with the referral services, get my name on the list of indigent counsel, and do whatever I could to open my own private practice.

"About a week before the wedding," she continued, "I found out just how much Owen was opposed to my plans. If the state's attorney hadn't been a good friend of my father's, I might never have known until it was too late, but Carl called and asked me to come into his office one afternoon. I was supposed to start working for him in about three weeks, so I figured all he wanted was to get a head start on the paperwork, being with a state agency and all."

Moisture filled her eyes. For what she'd lost? he couldn't help wondering. Or for what she'd saved?

"I learned that my small business loan had been turned down." Her voice caught and she pulled in a deep breath before continuing. "At the time, I couldn't understand what had gone wrong. Owen and I were getting married, he said he'd cosign the loan with me. Considering how opposed to my working he was, I took that as a good sign."

"He had no intention of signing for the loan, did he?"

"None," she said. "Apparently, Frank Cunningham, the loan manager, had mentioned the situation to Carl, and Carl put two and two together since there weren't any other young lawyers trying to start up a practice in Homer."

"Couldn't your father cosign for you?"

"Oh, sure, Dad would have done it in an instant, but that wasn't the point. Cunningham had said it would take about six weeks to get all the paperwork approved. I wouldn't have found out about the loan until *after* the honeymoon."

"So you called off the wedding."

She looked up at him, determination evident from a lesson learned the hard way. "Yes, and then I accepted a job with the Public Defender's office in L.A. I couldn't marry a man I didn't trust. If he was willing to go to those lengths to sabotage my career before he even had a ring on my finger, I can't even imagine what it would have been like after we said 'I do'."

He cut across the small terrace to stand in front of her. Gently, he reached toward her. "I'm sorry, Jill."

The grin she gave him was weak at best. "I am,

too," she said quietly. "Not because Owen and I didn't get married, but because of what I almost lost."

"Your career?" he asked, letting his hand fall to his side.

She shook her head, the length of her honey-blond hair floating over her shoulders. "Me."

Despite the hint of sadness in her voice, a grin tugged his lips. "It wouldn't have lasted," he told her firmly. Jill was too vibrant to allow herself to become lost in the shadow of anyone, let alone a man foolish enough to believe he could control her. "You're too tough to put up with that kind of control for very long."

"The funny thing is, I think I always expected Owen to issue an ultimatum. I just didn't expect it the way it happened."

"You almost sound like you have regrets."

"Only one," she admitted. "My decision brought the end to a twenty-year friendship."

He crossed his arms again and looked down at her. "You can't mean that. You couldn't have expected to remain friends with this guy."

"Oh heavens no. But Mrs. Kramer was probably my mother's closest friend until I called off the wedding."

Realization dawned, bringing with it another facet to her already complicated personality. Suddenly, he understood her taking such drastic steps to ensure she brought home the fabricated fiancé. She'd told him she didn't want to damage her grandmother's friendship with the grandmother of the guy she'd told she was already involved. Now he knew why she was convinced that would happen.

"Things happen for a reason, Jill. We don't know why one door closes until the next one opens, but you can't have regrets. And it wasn't your fault their friendship ended."

She flashed him one of those high-wattage grins that never failed to stir his blood. "Now you're sounding like my father."

Parental was the last thing he was feeling. "If I hadn't come home to take care of Raina and Will, Price Construction wouldn't exist today. How can I regret that?"

"You can't. And you have to consider your sister and brother. Your sister's going to be a nurse, right? She could be responsible for saving the life of a child, and that child could be the one to grow up and find a cure for AIDs or cancer or any other terminal disease."

"That's a little deep," he said with a chuckle.

She shrugged and stepped away from him. "I'm just saying you never really know what your purpose in life is all about. You might not be the one to finally bring world peace, but maybe someone you've touched in your daily life could. Just because I'm not like the rest of my family doesn't mean that my father's sermons haven't gotten through to me."

She stopped in the doorway to their room and turned to look at him. "Speaking of parents, mine adore you."

"I liked them, too." He walked toward her. "They're not exactly the way you've portrayed them."

"That's because you don't know them," she called

over her shoulder from inside their room. "They were on their best behavior tonight."

He chuckled and closed the door behind him. She honestly didn't see her parents in the same light. Her father was caring and kind, while her mother ran an enormous household with more efficiency than General Patton and more love than even he could imagine. Jill Cassidy was an apple that fell very close to the family tree, even if she wouldn't appreciate him telling her so.

She opened a dresser drawer, pulled out a floral scrap of satin material and flung it over her shoulder. "My sisters all like you. Even Ali. We won't talk about how you managed to charm my grandparents. You know you're the first future grandson-in-law that Granddad has actually said more than a dozen words to at any one time?"

He wondered what they'd all think of him when she told them they were no longer "engaged." Would she tell them a version of the truth? Use his own words that she was the wrong woman? The thought annoyed him, and he couldn't help wondering if she'd considered what she'd say to her family once they'd returned to L.A. and he was no longer a part of her life.

His heart gave an odd lurch at the thought of never seeing her again. "They're nice people, Jill," he said, hanging his lightweight jacket in the closet. "And they care about you."

She closed her eyes and shuddered dramatically. "They want me to be just like them."

She sat on the edge of the bed to slip off her low-heeled pumps and looked up at him. "How did you do it?" she asked, wiggling her toes. "You've managed to wrap every Cassidy in that house around your finger."

"You're more like them than you realize," he said quietly.

She moved toward the closet and glanced over her shoulder at him with a frown. "That statement alone just shows how much about me you *don't* know."

He eased up behind her, catching her gaze in the full-length mirror. "I know you've got your father's sense of humor," he said, sliding his hands down her arms. A slight tremble passed through her, and he grinned.

"You don't know him like I do."

"A lot of years of smiles and laughter gave your dad those deep laugh lines."

She shrugged, a barely perceptible lift of one slender shoulder.

He wasn't buying her noninterest. "I can also see all that determination and drive comes from your mother."

"Not likely."

Her gaze locked with his and she leaned against him, her backside pressed intimately against him. Heat shot south and burned.

The rules he'd established for himself were only as good as his ability to keep them. His didn't stand a chance of survival against Jill's sensual arsenal. Sliding his hands further down, he entwined their fingers. "You've got your Grandmother Shirlee's slender hands," he said, lifting one to his mouth to gently brush his lips over her knuckles.

She sucked in a sharp breath. Desire swirled in the depth of her eyes, further heating his blood.

"Your eyes are the exact same shade as your Grandmother Lydia's, and that little quirky thing you do with your nose when you don't like something is the same thing your granddad did when Dean passed him the broccoli."

"Those are...physical," she said in a voice barely above a whisper. That one word spurred his senses as he thought of all kinds of interesting ways to get physical with Jill.

"I also know you adore all of your sisters," he said, attempting to concentrate on their conversation and not the way her bottom rubbed enticingly against his fly. "You're close to Brenda and especially to Carly and Ali. And you've got a soft spot for kids."

She turned her head to the side, exposing the slender column of her throat. *Just one taste.*

"They're my nieces and nephews. Of course I have a soft spot for them."

One taste led to two. "You gush over babies," he whispered against her ear.

"You're wrong."

He chuckled, then nipped playfully at her lobe. "Of course you don't. That's why every time Francesca so much as whimpered, Aunt Jilly was the first one to pick her up and hold her."

She made a sound that could be taken for denial, or a moan of pleasure as his tongue trailed a path over her collarbone.

He opted for pleasure.

"But there's one thing I don't know," he said, lifting his head to look at her in the mirror. "Who is the real Jill Cassidy? Is she the tough lawyer I saw in the courtroom? Is she the sensual woman who propositioned me with a no-strings affair? Or is she a mystery that will take me a lifetime to solve?"

A slow grin eased across her lips, so seductive, so sweet. She turned in his arms. For a fleeting instant he thought about stopping before things went too far. His nobility wavered the instant she slid her hands upward over his chest to wind her arms around his neck.

"Right now she's the woman who wants to make love to you."

9

MORGAN'S QUICKSILVER gaze filled with desire, causing Jill's heart to flutter beneath her breast. Anticipation hummed between them as she narrowed the small distance until her body pressed against the granite hardness of his. He teetered on the brink of surrender. She felt it clear to her toes, along with another more dangerous emotion she refused to identify as anything but lust, regardless of the other *L* word her conscience kept pressing her to admit.

She sifted her fingers through the hair brushing the collar of his dark-blue cotton shirt. "I'll be gentle, I promise."

A trickle of hope pulsed in her veins when his mouth quirked into a brief smile. "I don't think there'll be anything gentle about it," he said, his hands moving over her hips to cup her bottom.

He dipped his head, his tongue teasing the shell of her ear. A delightful shiver eddied down her spine, bringing her state of awareness to full, sensual alert. Her pulse tumbled and careened when his lips skimmed along her jaw, then hovered just above her lips.

"Just one taste," he whispered.

The satin nightie she'd flung over her shoulder slithered to the floor, settling around her bare feet in a soft, cool puddle. If he didn't kiss her soon, satin wasn't going to be the only puddle on the floor.

"Just one," she answered, lifting her lips closer to his.

He hesitated for a brief second, his gaze searching her face. A groan ripped from his chest, and then his mouth caught hers in the sizzling kiss she craved.

His surrender fell into the category of delicious perfection. The heated kiss as demanding as her request, his tongue mating wildly with hers in an age-old rhythm that foretold of more seductive delights she couldn't wait to savor and explore. She moaned against his mouth and held him close, her senses scattered by the riot of sensations clamoring inside her.

She needed. Needed Morgan to fill the deep longing inside her.

She wanted. Wanted him with a desire that burned hot.

His mouth left hers, his tongue trailing down her throat to her shoulder. His teeth nipped at her lobe, at her collarbone, and she trembled. His hands eased up her back to her rib cage, his thumbs brushing the underside of her sensitized breasts, which were already straining against the satin cups of her bra. Restlessness shifted through her. She wanted him inside her.

Making love to Morgan would change everything, but she was beyond caring. She couldn't explain the connection between them any more than she could define her feelings for him. But it was there nonetheless, rooted in her being as if he was the one she'd been waiting for all along. The one man capable of making her believe that happily ever after didn't only exist in fairy tales, but for her. For them.

She'd make time for a relationship. No matter how much she cared about her career, the only briefs she was interested in at the moment were Morgan's, and seeing him slip out of them.

He backed her up until her spine brushed the wall. Using it to his advantage, he surrounded her with his body and his heat. The feel of his chest pressing against her breasts nearly drove her mad. She cursed the satin, silk and cotton separating their skin, wanting nothing less than heated flesh against heated flesh.

She craved.

She needed.

She wanted him.

Now.

Taking both of her hands in one of his, he lifted them just above her head. Her breath hitched in her throat at the sin-filled grin flirting around the edges of his mouth. With excruciating slowness, he undid the four buttons down the front of her blouse, then eased the top aside. "Red," he murmured, that rascal grin deepening as he hooked his finger around the front closure of her red satin bra. "It had to be red, didn't it?"

His gaze locked with hers as he flicked open the closure. "This wasn't supposed to happen," he said in that deep voice she'd never grow tired of hearing. "We weren't supposed to surrender under our rules of engagement."

"Let's just call it fate and not look beyond that," she told him quietly. "Besides, what's a few broken rules between...lovers."

He groaned in surrender and his fingers gently

pushed aside the cups of her bra, his gaze straying to her freed breasts. "God, you're so beautiful."

Her feminine pride inched up the scale at the awe in his whispered praise. Words died in her throat when he dipped his head, pulling one taut nipple deep into his mouth. She closed her eyes and arched toward him.

"I need to touch you," she managed around the soft moan building in her throat. She tried to tug her hands free. He added slight pressure to the gentle grip, then paid equal attention to her other breast while he fumbled with the button of her black slacks.

The rasp of her zipper sang in her ears, each notch adding to her already heightened awareness. He pushed the silky fabric first over one hip, then the other until it pooled around her ankles. She stepped out of her slacks and kicked them aside, the cool air from the air-conditioning brushing against her heated skin.

His hand slid over her stomach, down her abdomen, finally coming to a stop at the lace edge of her panties. Heat and need intensified when the tip of his finger teased and dipped beneath the lace. Desire exploded inside her when he slipped his hand past the satin to cup her heat in his hand.

She wanted to touch him, but he held her prisoner, not only with his hand holding hers above her head, but with each honeyed stroke of his fingers intimately against her. Her head spun, her senses scattered, her body arched toward his, seeking release from the tense need coiling tighter inside her.

"Go with it," he murmured against her mouth. "Come for me, Jill."

"I'd rather come *with* you," she gasped in a breathless whisper.

His lips sought hers again and he kissed her with that slow, thorough and sensual rhythm. He stroked her, with his fingers and his tongue, until she fell apart in his arms.

Slowly, she came back to earth. Her heart pounded heavily beneath her breast and her knees felt weak. Instead of languid and relaxed, she wanted more. More of him. All of him.

"I want to feel you inside me," she said, placing teasing nips along his jaw. "Deep inside me."

He groaned and released his gentle hold on her hands. "That's a very tempting offer," he said, placing a light kiss on her lips.

Stunned, she stared up at him. Regret filled his eyes. Regret that he'd allowed things to go so far, or that he refused to take their lovemaking any further?

"But?" Feeling exposed, physically and emotionally, she gathered her blouse around her, shielding herself as much as possible with the short silk top. "But what, Morgan?"

"But we can't."

"*Can't?*" she shot at him, angry, frustrated and way too emotionally charged. How could he not? Her gaze dipped to the contrary evidence straining against the cotton fabric of his trousers. Oh, he wanted her, all right. "Or *won't?*"

He reached for her and she sidestepped him. He let out a frustration-filled sigh and looked at her, that damned regret clouding his eyes. "I want you so much it hurts," he said gently, "but I have no way to protect you."

The argument hovering on her lips died. She couldn't argue with him. Not about something so important, even if awareness continued to vibrate through her in soft, gentle tremors. Homer wasn't L.A. with its twenty-four-hour drugstores and convenience stores. They had no choice but to wait.

She nodded briskly, stooped to pick up her nightie and headed into the bathroom without another word. He was right. They couldn't make love without protection. Why hadn't she thought of that? Where was it written that the man was the one responsible for those important little details?

She'd practically begged him to make love to her. She'd been the one to proposition him! How could *she* have forgotten something so important?

First errand on her agenda tomorrow morning: drugstore. Until then, she had a sinking feeling the night was going to be a very long and very restless one.

JILL CUT THE ENGINE but remained seated behind the wheel of the rental car, her gaze locked on the closed door to the cottage. Four more nights. That was all they had left. Once they returned to L.A., they'd resume their lives as if nothing special had ever occurred between them. Her gaze dipped to the gaily wrapped gift package on the seat beside her, along with the foam containers holding the light breakfast she'd picked up from the local diner.

So why was she hesitating when this was exactly what she'd wanted?

The answer evaded her.

Just as she'd suspected, sleep had been elusive.

Every time the bed shifted under Morgan's weight, she woke, and craved the man sleeping next to her. By seven-thirty, she gave up hope of getting anything more restful than a series of unsatisfying catnaps, and showered and dressed for the long day filled with prewedding activities. When Morgan had slipped into the shower, she'd left him a note telling him she'd gone into town for breakfast and would return soon.

She'd not said a word about the other stop on her agenda.

Pursuing a man was new to her, so she had no idea if she was doing it correctly. The Cassidy girls hadn't been allowed to call boys, so even when she'd gone off to college, she'd never asked a guy out on a date. They'd been taught by their mother that the thrill of the chase was what boys really wanted.

She took a deep breath then pulled the key from the ignition. Since most of the boys in Homer were afraid to call the daughters of the local preacher, it was a miracle she and her sisters even dated when they were in high school.

With a firm shake to her suddenly cowardly thoughts, which did nothing to still the heavy pounding of her heart, she slid from the vehicle, taking her gift and their breakfast of warmed croissants, homemade blackberry jam and fresh-cut melon with her. Was she coming on too strong? Would Morgan appreciate her gift or think she was too easy?

"Oh, get over yourself," she mumbled as she climbed the wooden steps to the cottage. Forever wasn't an option. For either of them. Why was she wasting time worrying about what Morgan thought of her beyond the next four nights? Four nights of blissful pleasure they both wanted. All she was doing was taking care of one tiny detail so they could enjoy what time they did have together.

So why did she feel as if her decision to buy a box of condoms meant so much more? There was nothing monumental about it. They wanted each other, and all she'd done was take the necessary steps to remove cold showers from their nightly routine.

Keeping that thought at the forefront of her mind, she opened the door and stepped into the cottage.

Morgan glanced up from the copy of the *Chicago Tribune* spread over the small round table in the corner of the room, a mug of coffee from the in-room coffeemaker clutched in his hand. A heart-stopping grin tugged his lips when he looked at her.

His black hair was still damp, combed away from his chiseled features. A pair of jeans hugged his strong thighs, and a stark white polo shirt emphasized that wide chest she couldn't wait to explore with her hands and her lips.

"Good morning," he said, way too cheery for someone who'd tossed and turned just as much as she had during the long, sleepless night. "I made us some coffee."

She carried the foam containers to the table. "Breakfast. And a *piece* offering," she added meaningfully. Her hand trembled slightly when she held the box toward him. No turning back now, she thought.

He took the small wrapped box from her and turned it over in his hands. "A peace offering?"

She let out a long puff of breath, then focused her

attention on clearing the newspaper from the table as if it was suddenly the most important task in the universe. "After what happened last night, it's the least I could do."

She glanced up in time to see the suspicious glint in his eyes. "Why am I suddenly afraid to open this?" he asked, testing the weight of the package in his big hand.

She laughed in a fraudulent attempt to mask her nervousness. "Just open it, Morgan," she said, taking the chair across from him. "It won't bite, I promise."

Slowly, he pulled the small white envelope taped to the top from the package, a light frown marring his forehead.

Her heart pounded while she served their breakfast on the paper plates the diner had provided. He tore open the envelope and slipped the card free.

"Very clever play of words, counselor," he said, his voice tinged with laughter. He flicked the plain white card with his thumb, the words *A piece offering, from me to you* printed across the face. "I don't think I need to open this to know what it is."

She hadn't been joking when she'd told him it was a "piece" offering. "I've never really liked cold showers," she said huskily.

His gaze darkened to a steely gray. "Neither have I." He reached across the small table and captured her hand. With a gentle tug, he drew her around the table and urged her to sit in his lap.

She needed no further invitation. With a smile filled with sin, she straddled his hips and slowly eased onto his lap.

"You make me want to forget about rules," he said,

settling his hands on her backside and urging their bodies closer together.

"What rules?" she whispered, wreathing her arms around his neck.

His hands slid over her bare legs, those incredible fingers teasing the top of her thigh just below the hem of her beige shorts. "Rules about a certain woman with different ideals and goals than my own."

She looked into his eyes, at the honesty banked in their depths along with something much more elemental that had her body humming with anticipation: desire.

"How do you know they're that much different than your own? You're making assumptions, Morgan, and that's not fair."

"Based on previous conversations, I'd call it fact."

She frowned and pulled her arms from around his neck. "What?" she asked, standing. "Because I refused to marry a man who only wanted to control me?"

Morgan let out a frustrated sigh when she moved away. He hadn't wanted complications, but somewhere between the night he'd agreed to pretend to be her fiancé and last night, when it'd taken every ounce of willpower he possessed not to make love to her, the rules of their engagement had not only blurred, they'd evaporated.

He wanted her, and regardless of their differences, he wanted more than just a long weekend of great sex with a woman who excited him and filled him with longing. He'd never made a habit of being dishonest with himself, and his conscience wouldn't let him deny the truth now. Jill was special, and she meant more to him than he'd expected. Whether or not they could make a relationship work, he didn't know, but if they had a chance of survival, then she at least deserved to know the reasons behind his doubts.

"I don't want to control you, Jill."

Her chin lifted in a show of defiance, frustration etched in her heavenly sapphire eyes. He couldn't blame her. He'd been leading her on an emotional roller-coaster ride, and that wasn't fair—to either of them.

She folded her arms over her chest. "Then what *do* you want?" she asked, her voice a little too sharp. "All I'm getting are mixed signals. Either you want me or you don't, Morgan. Make up your mind."

He'd spent the whole night wanting her. The urge to pull her beneath him and make her his had been so overwhelming, he'd very nearly given in and reached out to her. "I want you," he said quietly.

She narrowed her eyes. "Only until we return to California?"

He let out a sigh and stood. Crossing the room toward her, he considered his answer. He could agree with her and save them both the loads of heartache they were bound to endure. They were too different, or were they? "Now you're the one making assumptions."

"I have nothing else to go on," she argued. "Someone obviously hurt you, but I have no idea what happened. You won't tell me anything."

He should have known that simply because she hadn't brought the subject up last night, his past wasn't a closed topic. The look she'd given him in the car when they'd pulled up to the parsonage had said that the discussion was far from over.

He moved to the edge of the bed and sat. "I know what it's like to live with someone more concerned with her next promotion than her family."

"Because I called off the wedding to Owen, you're sticking me in the same category. That's not—"

"No," he said sharply. "What happened with you and Kramer, it's not even close. You didn't choose a career over a family, Jill. You escaped a bad situation before it turned worse. That's a clear-cut case of self-preservation, in my opinion. What I'm talking about is how my mother basically ignored her children. Her sole focus was her career and her own needs."

Her brows knit in confusion. Unless he dredged up the past and laid it before her, she'd never understand why he'd sworn off career women.

Until her.

"Not long after Will was born, my dad got caught up in a big budget cut at the university where he taught advanced English courses. His schedule was cut in half, so my mom had to go to work. She had her own degree in marketing, and landed a full-time job with an advertising agency. To be fair, the fault doesn't lie completely with Eleanor. Dad's ego suffered because his wife had to help support the family, but Eleanor's career just kept growing with one promotion after another until the bitterness between them had all but destroyed their marriage. After a couple of years, Dad's work picked up again, but by that time she was a V.P., something she refused to give up."

She moved to the bed and sat beside him. Slipping

her hand over his, she laced their fingers together. "And you blame her for this?" she asked.

"Not like you think. I'd never condemn anyone for following their dreams, but we hardly ever saw her. She was usually gone before us kids were up in the morning, and even when she wasn't traveling, we rarely saw her before we'd gone to bed."

Maybe if you took a little more interest—

That's not who I am.

Dammit, Eleanor, your children need you.

I provide for them.

And I don't, is that it?

I never said you weren't a good father.

Just not much of a provider, right?

He shook the memory from his mind. "I'd hear them arguing," he admitted. "Raina and Will were too young, but I remembered what it had been like before. Believe it or not, we weren't all that different from your family. But it all changed. Every night I'd pray they'd just get it over with and hoped that one of them would file for divorce."

She gave his hand a gentle squeeze. "Your prayers were answered."

"Oh yeah, they were answered, all right," he said with a wry twist of his mouth. "I was eleven. My mother came home from work early one night two days before Christmas. The four of us were putting up the tree, and I remember thinking that I hadn't seen her look so happy. I hadn't seen her smile like that since Will was born, and for a brief instant I hoped that maybe things were going to be like they'd been."

"But you were wrong?"

"She'd barely set her briefcase down when she announced we were moving to California. She was the one responsible for one of those fast-food jingles that was making the company tons of money, and as a reward, she'd been given a big promotion to head up some department in their Los Angeles office. Dad didn't even hesitate. He just refused. They said some pretty horrible things, and finally she left. We didn't see her again until she came back to take us to California six months later."

She moved off the bed to crouch in front of him. Gently, she lifted her hand and cupped his cheek in her soft, warm palm. "I'm sorry, Morgan."

Covering her hand with his, he entwined their fingers. "It was a long time ago."

Compassion lit her gaze. "Divorce is hard on everyone involved, but especially the kids."

He laughed, a trace of the old bitterness in his voice. "It was hard on us, but not on Eleanor. She didn't want us, Jill. She'd made that perfectly clear. The only reason she fought so hard for custody was because she wanted to punish my father. She was a success and she wanted to prove to him that she could have it all."

"But she raised you," she argued in defense of the woman who'd used her children to hurt the man who'd dared to refuse her. "That has to count for something."

"She paid someone to look after us," he said, his voice harsher than he'd intended. "Eleanor couldn't be bothered. We didn't have a mother. We had a live-in housekeeper who barely spoke English. Isabella taught us Spanish, and we taught her English. We had some interesting conversations."

Jill sighed, then settled to her knees and smoothed her hands over his thighs. "It sounds to me like not all of your memories are bad ones."

He slipped a lock of honey-gold hair behind her ear. "No," he admitted with a brief shake of his head. "Not all of them. But my point is those memories should've been with my folks, not a housekeeper we had to teach English so we could communicate.

"I've seen too many marriages fall apart. Half my crew is divorced, and it's always the same thing—they wanted different things. People grow apart, Jill, and the kids are the ones who suffer."

"You think I'm that shallow, is that it?"

"I did at first," he admitted. "But the more I get to know you, and your family..." He let out a sigh. "I'm not blind, Jill. You're nothing like Eleanor. There's a goodness inside you she lacked. You say your career's important to you, and I don't doubt for a second that it is, but I've seen the way you interact with your sisters' kids. That's something I rarely saw my mother do. She loved us, at least I like to think she did, in her own misguided way, but she lacked maternal instincts. She provided, she didn't nurture."

Jill slowly rubbed her palms rhythmically over his thighs and looked up at him with one of those electric grins. "Are you suggesting we explore the possibilities of a relationship?"

He settled his hands on her shoulders, smoothing his thumbs over the warm silky flesh exposed by the cotton scoop-necked top. "You make me want to forget about my iron-clad rules to avoid career women. I want you, Jill. I want you so bad I'm in a constant state of arousal. But it goes deeper than just wanting to have sex, because I want that emotional connection with you that goes beyond the physical aspects of a relationship."

She laughed nervously. "All this from a box of condoms?"

He dipped his head and tasted her lips in a quick, hard kiss. God, he wanted her. Thanks to her early-morning shopping trip, there was nothing to stop them from enjoying what they both wanted. "Let's just see where this leads."

Her grin faded. "What if it leads us somewhere we're not ready to go?" she asked, concern lacing her sweet voice.

Morgan shrugged. He didn't have an answer. The one thing he did know was that he'd gotten more than he'd ever bargained for when he'd agreed to play her fiancé. "Then we'll deal with it when and if it happens," he hedged, keeping his suspicion to himself.

A suspicion that included forever.

10

"I FEEL ABSOLUTELY ridiculous," Carly complained, plucking distastefully at the skirt of her wedding dress. She looked over her shoulder to her reflection in the full-length mirrors covering the back wall of the dressing room in Barb's Bridal Shoppe. "I look like a giant roll of wrinkled toilet paper."

Ali laughed and crossed the dressing room. "You look gorgeous, you little twirp," she said, coming up beside Carly, humor in her voice. She slung her arm over Carly's shoulders. "Like a blushing bride is supposed to look."

"You could be wearing this." Chickie held out the full skirt of one of the deep pink bridesmaids' gowns hanging on a large brass hook. "Do Ginger and Kay know their best friend plans to make them look like a pair of Pepto-Bismol bottles?"

Jill swatted Carly's hands. "Stop fussing," she ordered. "Ginger will look adorable in just about anything. I'm worried about Kay and all that gorgeous red hair carrying off the color, though."

"You know who's going to look gorgeous, is Janice," Carly said, smoothing her hands over the wrinkled skirt. "She's pregnant, and that soft pink for the matron of honor's dress just makes her glow."

"Leave it be, Carly," Jill scolded her sister again when Carly shook the skirt of the dress.

"Janice isn't the only one who'll be glowing," Ali blurted.

Jill's hand stilled. "Glowing, Al? As in now we know why you've been so moody?"

"We just found out." Ali smiled as her sisters surrounded her with hugs and well-wishes.

"This thing weighs a ton," Carly complained, stepping back on the dais a few minutes later. "I don't even want to think about what it's going to feel like with the stupid train."

"You're the one who wanted a big wedding," Ali said, turning to fluff the netting of the veil perched on a velvet-topped stand.

"No, I didn't." Carly shot Ali a brief glance. "Dean wanted this circus. I would have been happy sneaking off to Atlantic City."

Chickie gently slipped one of the bridesmaids' dresses back into its protective covering. "Dad would never have forgiven you."

Carly sighed. "I thought this was my wedding. And what's wrong with eloping? Am I the only one here who thinks it's romantic to sneak away in the middle of the night with the man of your dreams?"

"Chickie's right," Jill said, her thoughts slipping to Morgan. Was *he* the man of her dreams? The answer spooked her. "You'd break Dad's heart if he couldn't walk you down the aisle."

"Don't feel bad, Carly," Chickie said, puffing up the sleeves of the other dress. "Even Jill's going to have to endure all this fuss eventually. Speaking of which, when are you and Morgan going to set a date?"

Jill kept her gaze riveted on the folds of Carly's dress, carefully arranging the white satin over the crinoline. "We haven't discussed it," she answered evasively.

They'd discussed a lot of other things, things she hadn't expected. Why of all the men she knew did she have to pick the one guy with a conscience? Any other man would have jumped at her offer of an affair without the benefit of a commitment. But not Morgan. He practically demanded a commitment, even if in the next breath he claimed he didn't want one— with her.

She made a small adjustment to the dress, then carefully smoothed her hand over the tiny seed pearls. Ali gasped, then snagged her hand. "Where's your ring?" she demanded, holding Jill's hand up for Carly and Chickie's inspection. "She's not wearing a ring."

Don't panic. She hadn't even thought about a ring. She hadn't thought of condoms, either, so why should a ring have entered her mind?

"Oh, I...uh, left it at home. By mistake," she added quickly. Too quickly, judging by the suspicious glint in Ali's gaze.

"You left it at home?" Chickie parroted incredulously. She covered the last bridesmaid dress in the protective covering before turning to look at Jill.

Jill tugged her hand from Ali's grasp. "I was...uh, I forgot it, okay? What's the big deal? It's just a ring."

"An *engagement* ring, Jilly," Chickie said. "Not *a*

ring. And Morgan doesn't look like the kind of guy who'd be too happy about you forgetting his ring."

After what she'd learned this morning, she was positive he'd be very unhappy. But there was no ring, she reminded herself. How could there be when they weren't even engaged? They weren't...anything, other than wildly attracted to each other, and more than a little cautious when it came to taking that next step in their relationship.

What relationship?

Jill frowned. After everything he'd told her this morning before her sisters had arrived at the Village Inn to pick her up for Carly's fitting, she was even more confused. Her analytical mind had trouble putting it all into proper perspective. They wanted each other. That fact had been established before they'd even arrived in Homer, and had only intensified with each passing hour. Morgan suggested they just let their relationship develop.

What relationship? she wanted to scream.

She wasn't certain where they stood, except they were no longer on opposite sides of a wide chasm. Somewhere along the way, they'd reached a very precarious center. The only thing left was to take that final step—together.

All that kept her from taking that step was the fear that they'd tumble into dangerous territory.

"He is one gorgeous hunk of man," Carly said, dragging Jill's thoughts back to the present.

Ali lifted the ten-foot train from the protective tissue wrapping and helped Chickie attach it to Carly's dress. "If you go for those testosterone overload types."

Jill shot Ali a heated glance. "He is not a...one of those."

The three of them stood back and admired the bride. "Oh, Carly," Jill whispered. "You look absolutely beautiful."

Carly rolled her eyes. "I look like—"

"A giant roll of wrinkled toilet paper," Ali and Chickie finished in unison.

"Barb just needs to have the dress pressed and you'll be absolutely perfect," Jill pointed out.

"Back to Morgan," Carly said, stepping from the raised platform. "I don't think he's too macho."

Chickie snagged the pincushion from the low table. "Turn around, Carly," she instructed. "Morgan seems like a good man."

But so did Owen. No one said the words, but Jill heard them nonetheless. She'd been fooled once before; she wasn't about to repeat history. At least Morgan was honest, telling her up front that he had doubts because of her career.

Chickie slipped a few pins into the sides of the bodice, then ushered Carly back to the dais. "This hem needs a little work," she said, pulling over the padded velvet stool to sit. "I think Morgan is just what you need, Jill."

"I don't *need* anything."

"Oh Jill, stop it," Ali said, readjusting the satin train behind Carly. "We've all seen the way you two look at each other. If that's not love, I don't know what is."

"I should hope so," Chickie added. "They are engaged."

Guilt bit hard into Jill's conscience, and she fought

against blurting out the truth. She thought about the fifty-year friendship between Luther's grandmother and her Grandma Shirlee, and kept silent. Although she'd never be comfortable with the lies she'd told her family, after what had happened to her mother and Mrs. Kramer when she'd called off the wedding to Owen, she refused to be the cause of another long-standing friendship coming to an end.

"Just because they're engaged doesn't necessarily mean anything," Carly said in a quiet voice.

Three pair of eyes filled with varying degrees of surprise and curiosity shifted abruptly to the youngest Cassidy.

A deep blush covered Carly's cheeks. "What I meant was," she explained, "Jill was engaged to Owen and she really wasn't in love with him. Right, Jill?"

Chickie tugged on the hem of Carly's gown. "Let's not travel down that road, shall we?"

"Good idea." Ali moved to one of the rose velvet chairs and sat. Adjusting the floral skirt of her cotton jersey dress, she gave Jill a look filled with intent. "I'd rather find out how you two met."

"Through work," she said, handing Chickie the tape measure she'd signaled for. "He..." He what? Agreed to compound a lie? "He retained me to defend one of his employees on a minor charge."

"Is he romantic?" Carly asked in a wistful tone.

Jill crossed to the matching velvet settee. She thought for a moment. Morgan didn't strike her as the type to shower a girl with flowers and candy. Something practical, like maybe taking her car to the shop for an oil change, was more his style. Or bringing her dinner because she had to work late, she thought with a private smile. "In his own way," she admitted.

Chickie made a few adjustments to the hem of Carly's wedding gown. "Is he supportive?" she asked around the pins in her mouth.

"If you're asking me if he'd pull something low and underhanded like Owen did, then the answer is no," Jill answered. "Morgan's supportive, but..."

But, she had a few doubts, too. Not that he would ever do anything remotely close to what Owen had, but she did have doubts that he could accept her *and* her career as a package deal for something more long-term. She was dedicated to her profession, but she also knew and understood the importance of family. The fact that she'd allowed hers to believe a lie for all these months, no matter how misguided her attempts to protect them, showed just how much family meant to her. She'd never give up the law, but she didn't think Morgan would ever ask her to choose.

After what he'd told her about the unpleasantness of his childhood and all the failed marriages he'd witnessed as an adult, she had to admit his reluctance to take her up on her no-strings offer touched her in that silly place where she still believed in knights in shining armor.

"But?" Ali prompted, demanding her attention, for which Jill was thankful considering the dangerous path her thoughts had taken.

"But he feels like I do," she said, looking up at her sister. "Family needs to be first priority."

Morgan's words from the previous night stuck in her mind. He'd said she wasn't all that different from

her sisters. Could there be some truth to that statement, too?

No. She *was* different. Unlike her mother, who'd
passed up a promising medical career, Jill had refused to give up the law. While her sisters lived
within the city limits of their home town, with the exception of Lisa who lived four hours away, she'd
been the only one to move far from home. What she
didn't know was if her differences stemmed from
some mutant rebellion gene, or from the fact that
she'd been more scarred by Owen's control than
she'd wanted to admit.

"How do you know you're really in love?" she
asked suddenly. "How do you know he's the right
one?"

Carly's eyes widened in surprise, followed by a
fleeting glimpse of panic Jill was certain she imagined.

Chickie grinned. "Suffering from a little lingering
I-almost-married-the-wrong-guy syndrome?"

"Maybe," Jill admitted with a shrug, not willing to
examine too closely the real purpose behind her question.

Ali let out a slow breath. "You just...know."

"How'd you know Brad was the right one?" Carly
asked Ali.

A soft smile tugged Ali's lips. "He wouldn't leave
me alone. He kept showing up all the time."

Jill leaned back into the soft velvet, pulling her legs
beneath her. "You worked for him, Ali," she said.
"Of course Brad was going to keep showing up. He
owned the place."

"No," Ali said, grinning. "I mean he kept coming

up with these really lame excuses to hang around the office when he should have been out working on jobs or doing estimates."

Carly looked over her shoulder at Ali with a frown. "*That's* how you knew?"

Ali's grin deepened. "When he stopped, I missed having him around. Then I was the one coming up with lame excuses to get him into the office."

Chickie stretched her long legs out in front of her and leaned back on her hands. "Brenda said Paul wrote her a sappy poem."

"How'd you know with Sean?" Jill asked Chickie.

A grin tinged with wickedness canted Chickie's lips. "He had to go out of town on a job, and he called me every night for two weeks."

"How sweet," Carly said.

Chickie fanned herself as if she was suddenly hot. "Sweet isn't quite the word I'd use."

"Marilee!" Ali looked at Chickie with mock severity. "Are you saying you failed to conduct yourself like a lady?"

"Oh no, Al," Chickie said with a laugh. "Sean had no doubt I was every inch a lady after those phone calls."

Jill swallowed a giggle. No one could ever call Chickie shy.

Chickie sat up straight and urged Carly to turn slightly. "Mom said Dad wrote her a song."

Ali's jaw dropped, then snapped shut. "You're kidding! Dad?"

"I think it's sweet," Jill said. Somehow Morgan didn't strike her as the poetry-writing, ballad-penning type. No, whatever was on his mind, he'd tell her. Of that much she was certain.

"According to Mom, Dad was very much the romantic," Chickie commented, "and the absolute worst songwriter. She said if a man was that willing to humiliate himself, then it had to be true love."

Jill frowned. "But what about her career? Do you think she regrets not pursuing it?"

Chickie shrugged. "She's never talked about it."

Jill sat quietly while Chickie made the last few adjustments to Carly's dress. Her mother had thrown away a promising career in medicine to become the wife of a small-town minister. She'd almost made a similar mistake, but thankfully, she'd escaped before it was too late. "What about you, Carly? How'd you know Dean was the one you wanted to spend the rest of your life with?"

Carly stared at her reflection, her turquoise gaze filled with panic.

Jill stood and crossed the room to her sister. "Good grief, Carly, you're as white as your dress. Are you okay?"

Carly shook her head and reached out blindly toward Jill. "I can't breathe," she said, coming off the platform in a rush.

"You'll be fine," Chickie said, quickly moving to Carly's side, guiding her toward the settee.

Carly gripped the curved edge, her fingers pressing hard into the rose velvet until they turned white. "I think this corset thing is too tight. Jilly?"

Jill hurried to her sister's aid, working quickly to unfasten the dozens of pearl buttons down the back of the dress. Chickie helped ease the dress from

Carly's shoulders while Jill undid the fastenings of the restrictive undergarments. Ali slipped out of the room, then returned a few seconds later with a bottle of water.

Jill tossed a thin cotton robe over Carly's shoulders before her sister sank onto the velvet settee. With her arms wrapped around her middle, she leaned forward, taking deep breaths.

"You okay, Carly?" Chickie asked, pressing her fingertips to Carly's forehead. "You feel awfully clammy, kiddo."

Ali handed Carly the water, and she downed half the bottle. "I'll be fine," she managed around a brief smile that did nothing to lessen the panic still banked in her gaze. "I'm sure it's just all the excitement, plus I didn't have time for breakfast this morning."

Jill crouched in front of her sister. Smoothing back a thick lock of blond hair behind her ear, she asked, "Are you sure, Carly?"

Carly looked at Jill and nodded. "I'll be fine."

Jill worried, suspecting her sister wasn't being completely honest. Carly had never been overly dramatic, and something was definitely not right. The panic in her eyes, combined with the pale complexion and clammy feel to her skin, said "fine" was the last thing her little sister was feeling, and it was all too real to be anything less than an anxiety attack.

"Really," she said, offering a tremulous grin. "I'll be okay. I think I just need to eat something."

Not only real, Jill thought, giving Carly's hand a reassuring squeeze, but far too reminiscent of her own reaction to Owen Kramer's betrayal.

JILL SLIPPED the red satin chemise from the hook on the bathroom door, wondering if she'd made the right decision. While Chickie had been issuing instructions to Barb for last-minute adjustments to Carly's gown, she'd spied the lingerie section. Hanging on a padded hanger with a ridiculously expensive price tag was a whisper-thin red chemise she knew would have Morgan salivating. Without a second thought, she'd purchased the lingerie, making her hesitation now seem silly. Especially since she was the one who'd gone out and purchased the items necessary for a night of serious sin.

She slipped the garment over her head and let the material glide over her shoulders and past her hips. Perhaps her hesitation stemmed from the lessons she'd learned the hard way. Naiveté wasn't a badge of honor, and not something she wore well. She'd been foolish enough to allow herself to be taken advantage of once, personally and even professionally. A quick lesson in hardball had taught her how to play and win against some of the toughest lawyers the profession had to offer. Relationships hadn't been so simple, primarily because she'd been careful not to allow anyone to tread closely with any amount of seriousness.

Morgan was different. He was honest, goodhearted and equally confused about the attraction between them. Morgan Price *was* the quintessential nice guy.

She fluffed her bangs again, then started brushing her hair again. Chickie had been right. She was suffering from I-almost-married-the-wrong-guy syndrome.

Morgan had said they'd take things slow. Easing between the sheets with him, no matter how much she wanted him, fell drastically short of her definition of "slow."

After a day spent with family, wedding activities and visiting with relatives, they were finally alone.

She set the brush on the counter with a snap. She was stalling. If she fluffed her hair one more time or added another ounce of makeup, she'd look like a cheap floozy! With nothing left to postpone the inevitable, she took a deep breath and opened the bathroom door to the gorgeous hunk of man awaiting her pleasure.

11

MORGAN WAS THROUGH avoiding the truth. He wanted Jill regardless of his staunch belief that a woman with a career could never be a permanent fixture in his life. Tonight she'd be his, and he wanted her for a lot longer than the remainder of their stay in small-town America. He wanted her for as long as she'd have him, and then some.

He set the corkscrew he'd picked up at the liquor store along with a bottle of blush wine on the nightstand beside two motel-issue plastic cups. His afternoon search for a gourmet deli that sold fancy cheese, crackers and fresh fruit had him settling for the local market and Kraft cheese cubes, Ritz crackers and a plastic basket of strawberries.

Not exactly the fare for the romantic interlude he'd been planning all day, but it sure as heck beat beer nuts and Bud Light, which was about the extent of the liquor store's inventory.

The door to the bathroom finally opened. Morgan had been waiting nearly an hour for Jill to emerge. When he'd heard the shower running earlier, he'd summoned every fragment of what was left of his crumbled willpower to keep from slipping into the shower stall with her. Just the thought of smoothing his hands over her sleek curves and making her his had him uncomfortably hard.

He poked the cheese cubes with the last of the colorful cellophane-topped toothpicks, then turned to face her. His heart stopped, then slammed painfully behind his rib cage before resuming a frantic pace.

Jill, his own heavenly vision.

A heavenly vision in *red*.

"Wow," was all he could manage, and that sounded a little too much like a hungry growl.

Hungry? He was starved. For her. All of her.

She flashed him one of those high-wattage grins and moved slowly toward him, the satin clinging and moving against her curves at the same time. The curling edge of the hem brushed high on her thighs, and those glorious legs that had occupied his fantasies were bare and his to explore, inch by slow, tortuous inch.

"I take it that means you approve?" she asked in a sultry tone that made his heart beat faster and his palms sweat.

He swept his gaze over her curves, lingering on the tips of her breasts pressing enticingly against the clingy material. "The only thing better than this is bare skin," he said, continuing his perusal down that inspirational body, past the gentle curve of her hips, over her legs and back up again to the desire flaring in her eyes.

"I think I can arrange that." Keeping her gaze locked with his, she slowly dipped one shoulder until the thin strap of the sexiest piece of lingerie he'd ever seen fell halfway down her arm. She repeated the movement with the other shoulder until divine intervention was the only thing keeping the red satin in place.

As tempted as he was to flick the material with his finger to unveil all those dangerous curves, he had no intention of rushing her like some anxious teenager coaxing a girl into the backseat of a Chevy. He wanted her. All. Night. Long.

Reluctantly, he looped the thin straps loosely around his fingers. Slowly, he lifted them back in place, his hands skimming along her satiny skin. "I thought we'd have some wine first," he said, forcing himself to turn away from her.

"Morgan, you don't have to do this."

"Do what?" he asked, filling the plastic cups half full.

She took a cup from him with trembling fingers and glanced around the room. "Wine, cheese, soft lights." She cleared her throat. "I *want* to make love to you," she said in such a firm voice he couldn't help wondering if she'd been suffering with a few doubts of her own and needed to convince herself that making love wasn't going to be a mistake of monumental proportions.

"One glass," he said, gently urging her to take a sip.

She let out a slow breath and sat on the edge of the bed for about two seconds before springing back to her feet.

He bit back a grin. "You're nervous."

She shot him a quick glance over her shoulder on her way to the French doors. "Don't be ridiculous," she said, the haughtiness of her voice a poor mask for her sudden case of anxiety.

He took a sip of the wine and stood watching her. "Then why are your hands trembling?"

A brief smile touched her lips, and she let out a long sigh. "Okay, so I'm a little nervous," she admitted. "It's just... Never mind." She turned away to peer through the soft blue sheers covering the doors.

He set his glass on the nightstand and walked around the bed toward her. Taking the plastic cup from her grasp, he set it on the table, then took both of her chilled hands in his. "I've wanted you from the minute I saw you, Jill. That day I went to see Nick about helping Eddie, I couldn't get you out of my mind, and I didn't even know you."

Surprise lit her big blue eyes, and she flashed one of those secret female smiles that heightened a man's curiosity and did wonders for his ego. "You wanted me?"

"Yes," he said, smoothing his thumb over her wrist. "But I've been fighting it, and you. This won't be some brief no-strings fling, Jill. Are you prepared for that? Because if you're not, then this can't happen."

Her smile faded, replaced by a tugging of her brows as she searched his face. "But you said you wanted to take things slow."

"I didn't say anything about taking it slow. I said we'd deal with it when and if it happens. It's happening, Angel."

Something flared in her eyes, something that went beyond caution and headed straight into the territory named fear. A familiar emotion he understood all too well. He had his own share of fear when it came to an involvement with her that stretched beyond a make-believe engagement.

"You want a commitment?" she asked.

Frightening her away was not his goal, but he couldn't lie to himself or to her. Not now, not with something so important hanging between them. "I guess I do," he said quietly after a moment.

She tugged her hands and he let her go. "How exactly do you define commitment?" she asked, backing up a step.

He crossed his arms over his chest and looked down at her. A deer-in-the-headlights look warned him to proceed with caution. The pounding of his heart said he couldn't be anything but completely honest with her.

"A monogamous relationship. I don't know if this means forever, Jill. But it has to be a serious one-on-one. I won't accept anything less. I can't."

She didn't say anything, just kept looking at him with a combination of fear and surprise clouding her gaze.

He'd told her about his past so she'd understand how he felt. Considering her own previous relationship with a man foolish enough to want to control her, her apprehension made perfect sense, but he hoped she knew him well enough to know he'd never be anything but honest with her.

He closed the small space between them. Lifting his hand, he gently smoothed the backs of his fingers down her cheek. "I'll never lie to you, Jill. And I'd never do anything to hurt you."

"You can't make me a promise like that." She pulled back and looked up at him, her gaze ruthlessly direct. "You don't know what's going to happen in the future."

"I know that I care about you, and I want you in my life."

She slipped a lock of hair behind her ear. "You said you didn't want to get involved with a career woman. I'm not just a lawyer, Morgan. I'm an associate in a large firm, and that means long hours and late nights. When I'm preparing for trial, that's all that exists for me. Are you really willing to share me? Because that's what you'd have to do."

She wanted guarantees, and he couldn't blame her. "I want you, and all that goes with you. That's who I..." fell in love with? "It's a part of who you are," he said instead, and grinned. "That's the woman I want in my life, even if she does stand me up now and then."

A smile lurked around the edges of her very kissable mouth. He wanted to hold her, to promise her that it wouldn't matter in the long run, but he refused to give her false hope when he didn't have the answers. He understood and appreciated her drive and her need to succeed all too well. Those same traits had carried him through the lean times after Eleanor died. Jill was important to him, and he was more than willing to make an effort toward a lasting relationship, briefcases and power suits included.

"It's happening, Jill," he said again. "There's something between us that I can't explain, I only know it's there. Are you ready to see where it leads?"

With every second she hesitated, panic crept up his spine. He wanted her. Hell, who was he kidding? Regardless of how it defied logic, he *had* fallen in love with Jill Cassidy. He loved her laughter and her smiles, and she had a dozen variations. He loved the way her smooth-as-silk hair floated down her back and curled at the ends, or how her eyes told him exactly what she was thinking. He adored the way she curled her toes into the carpeting when she kicked off her shoes, and how she sighed with delight when she bit into a pastrami sandwich. He loved her openness and how she wasn't afraid to tell him exactly what she wanted. Her shyness earlier was nothing short of endearing.

"Yes," she whispered, her voice breaking with emotion. "I'm ready to see where it leads."

Profound relief ripped through him. He gathered her in his arms, holding her close to his heart—physically and emotionally.

"I won't hurt you, Jill," he said, smoothing his hands over her back. He caught the teasing scent of her perfume and something else, something much more basic that no perfume company could ever hope to capture. He breathed in the unique scent of Jill, and her need. "I promise."

She looked up at him, determination and desire replacing vulnerability and uncertainty in her eyes. "Shh," she whispered, tenderly placing her finger over his lips. "Just make love to me, Morgan."

The emotions he'd been fighting since she'd brazenly propositioned him swamped him. But he wouldn't drown. Not with his angel by his side.

He captured her hand before she pulled it away, tasting each one of her delicate fingers before gliding his tongue over her palm. Her eyes closed and she moaned, a sexy little sound in the back of her throat that had his blood pumping fast.

She eased closer, the cool satin covering her breasts sliding over his bare chest, shooting a blast of heat south. A sinful grin tugged her lips and she pulled her hand back, trailing her fingers lightly down his chest.

"I need to taste you," he said. "All of you."

He captured her lips in a deep, probing kiss, while guiding her toward the bed. Carefully, he eased them down to the soft mattress. He wanted to take things slow and easy, to savor each blissful moment of making her his. The need barreling through him when her hands skimmed over his chest and down his torso to the snap of his jeans had his control precariously close to disintegrating.

It didn't stop him from skimming his hand up her leg beneath the hem of her chemise.

His hand grazed her thigh, moving higher to her hip. When his fingers met with nothing but silky, smooth flesh, he moaned against her mouth.

She arched her back off the mattress, her hands working the zipper of his jeans. She ended the kiss, but used her tongue to tease his jaw, his throat, and finally his chest. Her mouth created a trail of heat that led straight to his already straining arousal. Her hands pushed his jeans over his hips, and before he could stop her, she held him hot and heavy in her slender hands.

"I want you inside me," she said, her voice a throaty purr that nearly brought him out of his skin. "Deep inside."

Words died in his throat at her sexy demand, and

his breath left him when her slim fingers wrapped around the length of his shaft.

"Angel," he rasped, when he found his voice. "We need to take it slow and easy." He attempted to shift his position, but she had other plans.

A sassy twinkle entered her eyes. She brought her other hand to her mouth, dipped her finger inside, then with aching slowness, circled the tip of his penis with the moist heat. "Is this slow and easy enough for you?"

He gritted his teeth and sucked in a ragged breath. God, he couldn't take much more.

She arched up off the bed and nipped along his jaw to his ear, her hot breath fanning his skin. He took advantage of the movement to shift their position, easing away from her hands, hoping to regain the few remaining fragments of his self-control.

He moved off the bed, then shifted her toward the edge before crouching in front of her. He smoothed his hands up the outside of her thighs, beneath the hem of all that red satin, to her hips. She reached for him again, and he grinned, easing her back down on the mattress. "Uh-uh, Angel."

He splayed his hands across her tummy, smoothing them down to the soft curls and the inside of her thighs. "Now it's my turn..."

Gently, he pushed her thighs open and settled her heels on the edge of the mattress. "To show you..." he said, brushing his fingers lightly over her feminine folds.

Her breath caught, and male satisfaction roared through him.

"My version..." he continued in a low voice, sliding his finger inside her moist heat.

She bit her lip but couldn't stop the soft moan from escaping.

With deliberate slowness, he retreated from her heated center and teased her the way she'd teased him. "Of slow..."

He blew a cool stream of breath against her heat, and she trembled. "And easy," he whispered.

Her hips moved, arching toward him in silent demand. She closed her eyes and tossed her arms carelessly over head. The granting of complete and total control tore through his heart. He knew what it cost her, and swore he'd never destroy the precious gift of her trust.

Ripples of heat purled across Jill's sensitized skin. The satin of her chemise rubbed against her nipples, intensifying the delicious way Morgan made her feel. Every part of her body felt alive with the sensuous heat vibrating through her.

His thumbs parted her and his warm breath brushed against her center. When he loved her in the most intimate way a man could love a woman, all she could do was feel. Feel the heat, the need and the tension coiling tighter and tighter inside her as Morgan pushed her close to the edge, then deliberately pulled her back just before she fell, carrying her to a new plateau of heightened awareness with each slide of his tongue or honeyed stroke of his fingers.

"Please," she cried when he held another orgasm just out of her reach, then pushed her forward again only to leave her dangling expertly until that last split second before he pulled her back yet again. Her legs trembled. Her hands gripped the edge of the mattress until her fingers ached. Her breath came in hard, short pants and sweat beaded on her forehead.

She'd never experienced anything like what Morgan was doing to her. She'd never experienced passion like this, so real and raw and emotional, so full of love.

She didn't have time to dwell on her emotions. Not with her body quivering with sensations unlike anything she'd ever known. Not with him pulling her along to the edge, teasing her, making her crazy with need, making her hot and wet and craving fulfillment, only to give her a glimpse of what he so expertly held just out of her reach.

He moved suddenly, and she opened her dazed eyes to watch him shuck out of his jeans and briefs. She stared in fascination as he sheathed his hard length in protection. He was beautiful, she thought, all muscle and sinew. And all hers.

Their gazes connected and held for several heartbeats. Her breath hitched in her throat at the stripped-bare emotion in his eyes. An emotion she'd carefully avoided for far too long. Love.

The realization failed to frighten her. Instead, she opened her arms and her heart to the one man truly capable of touching her soul.

Pleasure speared through her when he joined her fully on the bed. He pulled the satin from her, then let his hand trail over her body, touching her with such tender reverence her heart ached.

Her breath snagged when she looked into his gray eyes. "Make love to me, Morgan," she whispered in sensual demand.

A sexy grin tugged his lips. "Tired of slow and easy?"

Her pulse quickened with excitement and a need still unfulfilled. "I don't care how we get there," she said, pressing her lips against his hard, smooth chest. "Just take me there Morgan. Take me there and love me."

He answered her demand by moving over her, then settled back on his knees. He urged her hips forward until her backside pressed against his rock-hard thighs and her knees cradled his hips. He touched her with his fingers until she moaned from the intense pleasure assaulting her.

"You're so wet," he murmured in that deep velvet voice she'd always suspected was made for whispering in a woman's ear while they made love. "And hot."

She groaned and rocked her hips toward the pleasure, closing her eyes. She gasped as another rush of intense heat rumbled through her. Her senses went haywire as she made a vain attempt to catalogue the varying degrees of pleasure, the feel of his hard thighs pressed against her bottom, the glide of his fingers sliding deep inside her, and the heat of his sex pulsing against her.

He pulled back suddenly, shifting his legs until she was practically suspended, held in place only by her legs wrapped around his waist and his hands gripping her hips. He rocked forward, sliding his length slowly inside her, filling her. With his hands on her hips, he moved her far down the length of him, then away, slowly at first, then with more power, effectively building the tension tighter and tighter, forcing her higher and higher.

"Open your eyes, Jill" he demanded, his voice a tight whisper. "Look at me when you come, Angel. Let me see inside you."

Her world narrowed to just the two of them as she opened her eyes and looked at Morgan. Her heart swelled at the love shining in his gaze. The erotic dance of their bodies had her twisting the sheets in her fingers as the need built again, until finally he took her there.

Her back arched and her body vibrated with sensations too beautiful to name. Her release came hard and fast, slamming into her and carrying her over the edge with swift intensity, then holding her captive in sweet oblivion as tremor after tremor continued to course through her. She cried out, sobbing Morgan's name as her world dipped and swirled and then spun completely out of control as he continued to hold her suspended inside the whirlwind, never letting her fall back to earth, but keeping her in that sweet place where her body came alive just for him.

He shifted again, moving over her. She kept her legs locked around his waist and wrapped her arms around him and held him close, reveling in the length of his body finally pressed against hers. He moved against her, lifting her bottom and burying himself deep inside, over and over again, never allowing the delicious sensations to completely ebb.

A groan ripped from his chest as he gave in to the passion. She held him, smoothing her hands over the hills and valleys of his muscled back, pressing her fingers into the granite-hard flesh.

Moments passed with their bodies still locked together, and Jill cherished every second. The slow drift back to earth was as sweet as the rocket journey to the heavens. She loved the feel of his body beneath her hands, of the length of his body intimately aligned with hers, their hearts pounding in perfect rhythm.

He raised up on his elbows, his big hands tenderly cradling her face. The kiss was slow and deep. She tasted every emotion fueling that kiss, and knew she'd never really loved until this moment.

Until Morgan.

He ended the kiss and stared down at her. Her throat tightened and her eyes misted with emotion. "I love you, Morgan," she whispered before she could stop herself. The words felt foreign to her, new and untried, but too beautiful not to share.

His eyes darkened, and a gentle smile curved his mouth. "I know just how you feel, Angel."

Miracles came in all shapes and sizes. And so did love, she thought. Hers just happened to be six foot two with fierce gray eyes and a body made for sin.

12

MORGAN SWIPED at the steam-covered mirror again, before smoothing the razor down his cheek. Last time he looked, Jill was still sleeping soundly. He thought about waking her since they were due at the country club within the hour, but he just didn't have the heart to disturb her even if they were running late. The midnight sky had faded to the soft gray of early dawn before they'd finally fallen into an exhausted slumber.

He wanted her again, now, and didn't think he'd ever have enough of her. It was more than just sex. What he felt for Jill ran deeper than he'd been prepared for, but he realized now that whatever was happening between them had been inevitable. Fate was the only explanation he could find that made even the most remote amount of sense.

She'd not only stolen his heart, the sweet admission of her feelings for him had left an imprint on his soul, branding him for life.

The bathroom door pushed open, and his seductive, sleepy-eyed angel strolled into the small space, a sexy smile full of sass curving her lips.

"Good morning," she said, slipping up behind him to wrap her arms around his middle. Her cheek rested against his back, her warm breath fanning his skin. He hardened in a flash at the reflection in the mirror of her hands splayed over his abdomen. "Love your new outfit."

The outfit in question was a white towel slung low over his hips. "You looking for trouble, Counselor?" he asked, attempting to concentrate on shaving and not the way her fingers teased the knot holding the towel in place, or how his heart lurched in his chest at the sound of her low, seductive laughter.

"Is that what they're calling it these days?"

He flinched when the razor nicked his skin. The woman was trying to kill him.

She pressed her lips to his back while her hands fumbled with the knot.

"We'll be late," he warned, summoning every last shred of willpower to give her the opportunity to stop.

"So we'll be late," she said, trailing little biting kisses along his spine. "We'll show up smiling and everyone will wonder what we've been up to."

He chuckled and wiped away the remnants of shaving cream with a hand towel. "They'll probably have a pretty good idea of what we've been doing," he teased.

The towel circling his waist hit the floor and she moaned, that little sound that he loved hearing. Her hands slipped over his already throbbing length, and he closed his eyes as her fingers worked magic, making him impossibly harder in a matter of seconds.

She urged him to turn around and wreathed her arms around his neck, rubbing her satin-covered body against his while claiming his mouth in a hot, openmouthed kiss full of passion. He settled his hands on her hips and rocked her even closer, wanting, needing the feel of her curves against him.

She ended the kiss and looked up at him with a sinfilled grin and a heat-generating expression. With her gaze locked on his, she settled to her knees in front of him. His jaw clenched when her sweet breath fanned his erection. Her tongue flicked over his taut, tender flesh, and he sucked in a ragged breath. "Jill," he rasped.

"I need to taste you," she whispered, using his own words to taunt him.

He balled his hands into fists, fighting to hold on to the whisper-thin thread of control. He was afraid to move, afraid to breathe.

Her mouth closed over him. He gritted his teeth and groaned, a sound low and savage.

Unable to stand another minute of her delicious brand of torture, he hauled her to her feet and crushed her against him, claiming her mouth in a deep, soul-reaching kiss. Gripping her bottom, he turned and lifted her onto the counter, eased between her thighs, stopping only long enough to protect her before they came together in a wild explosion of heat, fired by passion, fueled by emotion and tempered in love.

ONE OF THE BENEFITS of a large family included work parties, and the Cassidy girls and accompanying husbands and fiancés, real or imagined, were in attendance to add the finishing touches to the country-club hall for the wedding reception. All that would remain were the flowers and greenery, which the florist would have in place the following day.

Jill handed Morgan a box filled with wedding favors. Her grandmothers had spent hours placing candy-coated white almonds inside small plastic wedding bells, then wrapping them in pink netting, tying them with satin ribbon and securing a miniature replica of Carly and Dean's wedding announcement. Glued onto the end of each ribbon was a delicate pink satin rose.

"This was a lot of work," Morgan said, holding up one of the favors for inspection.

"Didn't anyone ever tell you that's what grandmothers are for?" She set a favor at each place setting next to the linen napkins and fluted champagne glasses. "They've done something special like this for all of my sisters."

Male laughter drifted across the large dining hall, catching Jill's attention. Sean, Brad and Paul were busy filling helium balloons while Chickie, Ali and Brenda tied various shades of pink streamers to the ends, before letting them float to the ceiling above the parquet dance floor.

"You should be over there helping the other guys," she said, leaning across the table to place a favor on the opposite side. "Looks like they're having a good time."

"I don't mind." He leaned close, his body pressed along the length of her back. His warm breath, hot against her ear, sent a delightful shiver chasing down her spine. "Watching you bend over the table like this inspires me."

She bit back a smile. How did she ever get so lucky? she wondered. She hadn't believed she'd ever fall in love again, but who was she to question fate?

She pulled a few more favors from the box. "Again" didn't fit, she thought. Again meant that she'd been in love with Owen, and she realized now that what she'd felt for Owen hadn't been love. Affection, perhaps, but nothing remotely close to the deep-in-her-soul emotion she had for Morgan. With Morgan, happily ever after no longer existed in a faraway girlhood dream. Forever smacked of a reality she hadn't expected to find in the man she'd bartered her services to in exchange for a convincing facsimile of a fiancé.

"Jill?" he asked.

She glanced over her shoulder at him, and he inclined his head toward the glass wall overlooking an ornamental garden.

She straightened and watched as Carly said something to Dean, her body language tight and filled with frustration. His response was heated, followed by an equally heated reply from her baby sister.

"What are you two staring at?" Chickie called from across the room as Dean reached for Carly, but she pulled away.

Jill said nothing, but continued to watch her sister and Dean exchange more heated words the rest of them couldn't hear. The laughter and conversation in the room faded as the group saw Dean spin on his heel and storm off down the brick path toward the parking lot. Carly slowly sank onto the stone bench, her arms wrapped around her middle, looking small and alone.

Jill dropped the favors back into the box. "I'll be back," she told Morgan, then headed toward the garden.

Carly looked up with red-rimmed eyes as Jill approached. "It's just prewedding jitters," she said, her voice tight with emotion.

Jill sat next to Carly and slipped her arm around her shoulders. "Yours? Or Dean's?"

Carly let out a ragged breath and leaned against Jill. "Mine."

She should be the last person to offer premarital advice considering her own past. "Are you sure that's all it is?" she asked. After Carly's reaction during the fitting, Jill couldn't help but be concerned. She knew what it was like to be in a situation so out of control that finding a foothold to stop the spinning was an emotional roller-coaster ride in itself.

Carly nodded. "It's just all—" she spread her arms wide "—this. I really didn't want a big wedding, Jilly. But everyone's gone to so much trouble, not to mention the expense, and I don't..." She let out another ragged breath and shook her head.

"You don't what?" Jill asked quietly. *Don't want to get married?*

Carly sighed again and straightened. "Nothing," she said, with an obviously forced grin. "I'm just being silly. It's all a little overwhelming, is all."

Jill wasn't convinced. If her sister was going through with the wedding because she was afraid to call it off, then she'd end up miserable and married to the wrong man. She knew firsthand how difficult it would be, but if Carly wasn't ready, she needed to say something now, before it was too late. "Carly, if this isn't what you want, you need to tell Dean."

Carly shook her head and stood. "No. Dean's right," she said, swiping at the moisture clouding her vision. "It's just the jitters. I'll feel better tomorrow. I promise."

"Jill," Brenda called out, rounding the path. "There's a phone call for you. It's from L.A."

Jill frowned and stood, wondering what had gone wrong at the office for her secretary to call her here. "Are you sure you'll be okay?" she asked Carly, not wanting to leave her sister alone.

Her little sister gave her a tremulous smile. "I'll be fine."

"Jitters?" Brenda asked Jill in a low voice filled with concern.

"That's what she says," Jill answered, still unconvinced. "Stay with her, okay?"

At Brenda's nod, Jill reluctantly left Carly and headed toward the country club's kitchen area.

"Elaine?" she said into the receiver. "Is everything okay?"

"Jill! It's Nick. Enjoying your vacation?"

She frowned and checked her watch. It was a little after two in the afternoon on Friday in Homer, and two hours earlier in Los Angeles. Mentally, she flipped through her calendar. She hadn't had any court appearances for another associate to cover, so nothing could have gone awry in that area. "Yes, it's been nice," she told her boss. "Is something wrong, Nick?"

"No," he said with a chuckle. "No, nothing's wrong. In fact, I have good news for you. Real good, which is why I called."

Her frown deepened. "And?"

"Montgomery recommended you for a position that opened up unexpectedly. The other partners voted unanimously. Congratulations, Jill. You're now a senior associate, and second in command of the criminal law section."

A promotion? She'd only been with Lowell and Montgomery for two years. True, she'd worked hard, but a promotion had been the last thing she'd expected after such a brief period with the firm. Consistently, her monthly billable hours averaged over two hundred, attesting to the fact that she often put in twelve-hour days or longer. "I don't know what to say."

"Say 'thank you, Nick, for teaching me everything I know.'"

Jill laughed. "Thank you, Nick. This is a nice surprise."

"I hate to lose you, Jill. You're a damned good attorney. Bill Mitchell's a good guy. You'll like him and—"

Alarm skirted along her spine. Lose her? "Wait a minute," she said. "What do you mean 'lose me'? Is Mitchell transferring from San Francisco to replace you?" Nick was the head of the criminal law division for the Los Angeles office. Lowell and Montgomery consisted of four offices, with Los Angeles as the main office support for satellite offices in San Diego, San Francisco and Sacramento.

"No, Jill," Nick answered. "You'll have to relocate."

She closed her eyes and rested her forehead against the cool stucco wall. Relocate. To San Francisco. Four hundred miles away from Morgan. "I see."

"Is that a problem?" he asked without threat.

Not a problem, she thought. More like a catastrophe. "No," she lied, straightening. "It's just a surprise."

"This is a very good move for you, Jill. We'll talk more when you get back on Tuesday."

"Bye, Nick," she said, but the line had already gone dead.

She hung up the phone and walked slowly back into the hall. She got as far as the doorway and stopped. Morgan's back was to her, and he was setting favors on the tables.

Why now? Why now when she had everything she could possibly want? She couldn't turn down the promotion. She'd earned it, and the unanimous vote by the partnership said they believed she was worthy of the position.

If she took the job, she'd lose Morgan.

"Wham!" she muttered.

Once again she had everything right where she'd wanted it and then—*wham*—something came along to change her plans, slamming the door on her happy ending.

WITH A GRUNT of frustration, Morgan yanked out the knot of his tie for the third time. He couldn't concentrate, and blamed Jill since his attention kept shifting to her. Since she'd received that phone call this afternoon, she'd been oddly quiet. She'd said everything was fine, but considering his angel hadn't spoken more than a dozen words since they'd left the country club, he wasn't buying it.

"Tell me why I have to wear a tie again," he said, attempting once more to knot the silky fabric.

She slipped a thin gold hoop through her lobe. "Because it's traditional for the rehearsal dinner," she said, adjusting the second earring in place. "At least in my family, anyway."

He knotted the tie, but the large end hung past his belt.

"Let me," she said, crossing the room toward him. She wore a simple black dress that showed off her figure, and black strappy shoes. Red painted toenails peeked through her stockings. She looked elegant, and sexy as hell.

She adjusted the ends of the tie, then worked on the knot, her brow furrowed in concentration. She didn't chatter, she didn't smile, and he worried.

"Are you sure everything's okay?" he asked her again.

She finished with the tie, then slid the knot into place. She kept her hand pressed against his chest and looked up at him. Worry lined her eyes, making him dread her answer.

"Nick called," she said in a quiet voice filled with resignation. "He had some news that couldn't wait until Tuesday."

He frowned. "What kind of news?"

"A senior associate's slot became available. Mr. Montgomery recommended me for the position and the partnership voted in my favor."

There was no joy in her statement. No pride. Only that quiet resignation that filled him with dread and slipped something cold around his heart. "Why aren't you happier about it?" he asked cautiously.

Her hand slowly returned to her side. "Because it means I have to relocate to San Francisco."

That cold grip on his heart squeezed until his chest

hurt. He was losing her before they even had a chance. Just like his father had lost Eleanor with each progressive step in her career, he was losing Jill to the same demanding mistress.

"I see," he said, his voice harsher than he'd intended.

"I didn't know this was going to happen," she said, a defensive note in her voice. "I'm not even sure of all the details yet."

"But you've already accepted the job, right?" he asked in that same harsh voice. Something snagged his memory, a foggy glimpse of the past he couldn't quite see, yet sensed its presence in the mist.

She leveled him with her big blue eyes. "I can't turn it down. I've worked hard, Morgan. I deserve this promotion. Upward mobility within a firm the size of Lowell and Montgomery is usually slow. I'll be the youngest senior associate in the history of the firm."

"Congratulations, Counselor, on a job well done," he said a little too snappishly, then stepped around her to the French doors and swung them open.

"Thanks, Morgan. I can tell that really came from the heart. Your support astounds me."

Instead of arguing with her, he stepped onto the patio and breathed deep. He needed air, a lot of it.

Planting his hands on his hips, he looked up at the twilight sky. He supposed this was what he deserved for breaking his own rule. What had he been thinking? Of course her career would come first. He'd had an early lesson and he'd chose to ignore it, thinking Jill was different.

He'd been a fool. He'd given her his heart and

damned if she didn't trade it in for the next rung on the corporate ladder at the first opportunity.

"Why are you making this so difficult?"

Her soft voice drifted to him and he turned to face her. He could rant and rave, but knew his arguments would be futile, just as his father's had been. "I'm not trying to make anything difficult for you. I'm accepting reality. You're moving to San Francisco."

She stared at him with disbelief. "What are you saying? That if I take the job then it's over between us?"

"There can be no us if we live over four hundred miles apart. It won't work, Jill." Better to cut their losses now instead of attempting to make a long-distance relationship work, no matter how much it hurt him to let her go.

She narrowed the space between them and placed her hand on his chest, right over his battered heart. "Come with me."

A tempting offer, but one he couldn't accept. "My life is in Riverside. My home, my family, my company."

Her hand curled into a fist against his chest. "You can always buy another house," she said, a note of desperation in her voice that tugged at him. "Your brother and sister are both in college, so it's not like you'd be uprooting them."

"What about the company?" he argued. "What do I do about my livelihood? What happens to the people who depend on me for a paycheck?"

She stepped back and crossed her arms. "Can't you move the company to San Francisco?" she asked, that defensive tone back in her voice. "Or open a satellite office and run both from the Bay Area?"

"The company is too new to support expansion. I've got people depending on me, Jill," he said, feeling more than a little defensive himself. "I have an obligation to my employees, general contractors, not to mention Raina and Will. I'm all they have."

He had to get out of there. If he stayed, they'd only end up arguing, and he didn't want what was left of their brief time together to end with more hurt between them. He'd already had enough to last him a lifetime.

He brushed past her and strode to the closet for his garment bag.

"Where are you going?" she demanded, following him back into their room.

Their room? Tonight it'd be all hers.

"Back to L.A. Tonight."

"Morgan, you can't leave now. What—"

"Tell your family I had an emergency and had to return unexpectedly." He tossed the garment bag on the bed, then returned to the closet for his clothes.

"That's not what I meant," she said, her quiet voice ripping at his conscience. "How can you leave now, just when we…"

He finished packing the garment bag. She stood on the other side of the bed they'd shared, her eyes imploring him to stay, to work out a solution so they could be together. God, he wanted nothing more than to spend the rest of his life with her, but it would never work. For a brief time, maybe, but eventually they'd drift apart. Her career came first. She didn't say it. She didn't have to. He knew. Just as he knew she'd accepted the promotion without even discussing it with him first.

He circled the bed until he was standing in front of her. She looked up, the pain in his own heart mirrored in her eyes. He wanted to gather her in his arms and tell her they'd find a way to stay together, but he couldn't lie to her. The only way they could be together was if she'd give up the promotion, and he'd never ask that of her.

"I fell in love with you," he said honestly, laying open his heart to her. "I didn't expect it, but it happened. If we prolong the inevitable, it's only going to be harder to say goodbye."

"There has to be something we can do," she said, her voice breaking with emotion.

He settled his hands over her shoulders, smoothing his thumbs over her silky skin. "There is," he said. "Accept reality and move on. Your hard work is being rewarded, and I understand that. I'm not going to stop you from taking that promotion, Jill. I'd never do that."

"Maybe you haven't said 'it's me or the job,' but that's exactly what you're doing. If I take the promotion, then it's over between us. That's a pretty strong ultimatum, if you ask me."

"No, Jill," he said with a shake of his head. "I won't stand in your way. If you don't take this promotion, you'll eventually come to resent me. I won't be responsible for your unhappiness. You want this job, then take it. You've earned it."

He let his hands fall to his side, then turned to finish packing. She eventually moved to sit on the edge of the tapestry chair, quietly watching him prepare to walk out of her life for good. She didn't cry, but he could see she felt as miserable as he did. She didn't say a word to stop him, other than to tell him to take the rental car; she'd have one of her sisters take her to the airport on Monday.

With nothing left to do but leave, he gathered his bags. He wanted to hold her one last time, taste her lips, feel her body pressed intimately against his. He tightened his grip on his bags instead, afraid if he touched her, he'd stay and end up making them both miserable.

"Good luck, Angel," he said quietly, then headed for the door.

"Morgan?"

He stopped and turned, hating that he was the one responsible for the hurt in her eyes.

"What if I stayed in Los Angeles?" she asked. "What if this promotion didn't include a relocation?"

"We'll never know, will we?" he said, reaching for the door. "Because you're going to San Francisco."

13

UNABLE TO BEAR another second alone in the cottage with the memories of the time she'd spent with Morgan, Jill decided to walk the six blocks to her parents' house rather than call one of her sisters for a ride. She needed to be alone with her thoughts, and her breaking heart, but not here. Not where every square inch of the room reminded her of what she'd just lost.

The Friday evening was quiet, and thankfully she didn't have to share her solitude. The hour was too early for the local teenagers to flood Main Street or the pizza parlor in search of video games and a good time, and a little too late to find the more elderly residents of Homer sitting on their porches or out taking walks and enjoying the warm, sultry breeze.

By the time she climbed the back steps to her parents' house, a blessed numbness had settled over her. She'd hoped the walk would grant her a shred of relief from the physical reminders of two of the most wonderful days of her life, but despite the hollow feeling inside, the pain surrounding what was left of her tattered heart still ached.

She walked into the kitchen and found her mother, Lisa and Wendy busy with last-minute preparations for the elaborate buffet that would be set up in the dining room. The wedding party wouldn't be returning from her father's church for at least another hour. Soon family and friends would flood the house, and with a little luck, for just a few hours she'd be able to forget about the hurt in Morgan's eyes and the hardness of his features when he'd said goodbye.

"You're here early," her mother said when Jill set her purse on the chair. The warm smile gracing Marilyn Cassidy's still-beautiful face faded. "Jilly, are you okay?"

No. She'd never be "okay" again.

She propped her elbow on the counter and filched a carrot stick from the platter her mother was busy filling with raw vegetables. Jill laughed, but her attempt at humor sounded more caustic than comedic. "Do I look that bad?"

Lisa covered the fresh-baked rolls with a bread cloth and gave her a sharp look. "I haven't seen you look this upset since you whacked off Carly's hair. What's wrong, kid?"

"Nothing that won't heal with time," she muttered, dragging the carrot through the ranch dip.

Wendy arranged the casserole dishes on the oven rack and closed the door. "Where's Morgan?"

Jill glanced at the clock above the stove. "Probably about ten miles away from Chicago by now."

Three pairs of varying shades of blue looked at her expectantly.

He left me.

She blinked back the rush of tears burning her eyes. "He's gone back to California," she managed, her voice breaking. She tried to fight the tears, but nothing in her personal arsenal could wage war against a broken heart.

He'd not only left, she thought, he'd lied to her. He said he'd never hurt her, and he'd lied. He'd gone and taken her heart with him. No. That wasn't right. If he had taken her heart, then she wouldn't feel the damned thing shattering into a million pieces.

"Excuse me," she muttered, then hurried out of the kitchen. By the time she reached the staircase leading to the upstairs rooms, her vision blurred and the tears fell. She reached blindly for the banister and climbed one, two stairs, then dropped onto the carpeted step and buried her face in her hands.

Oh, how she hurt. She hurt so deep inside she doubted she'd ever fully recover. They were in a no-win situation and it was over. He said he loved her. If he truly did, wouldn't he have found a way for them to be together?

She felt an arm slip around her shoulders and urge her into an embrace. She breathed in her mother's soft cologne and didn't hesitate. She sobbed like a child, clinging to her mother for comfort. A colorful bandage on her "owie" wouldn't alleviate the pain this time. There'd be no gentle, "See, all better," and a kiss on the tip of her nose to make her smile and forget about the sting of a scraped knee or a stubbed toe.

Her mother whispered softly to her in that same soothing tone Jill had often turned to as a child, phrases that wouldn't help the hurt she felt now. Those were fine for broken dolls or a torn blouse, not a broken heart.

When her tears were spent, Jill straightened. "I'm sorry," she said, swiping at her face.

Her mother smiled gently and handed her a tissue. "It can't have been that bad of an argument," she said in that quiet, reassuring tone. "Morgan probably just needs a little time to cool off."

She wished. He hadn't been angry, just...resigned. She almost wished he had gotten angry. If he had, perhaps there'd be a chance of a future together, but other than a few abruptly spoken words, he'd been too calm, and too...accepting. As if he'd known it'd only be a question of time before her job would eventually come between them.

"He loves you, Jilly," her mother said. "Morgan wouldn't have asked you to marry him if he didn't."

Jill dabbed her eyes again with the tissue. They weren't engaged. They never had been. Guilt nudged in and joined heartbreak.

She pulled in a deep breath and gazed at the slash of light from the dining room spilling across the dark beige carpeting. She hadn't planned on ever telling her family she'd lied to them, but keeping up the pretense now seemed silly. Confession was supposed to be good for the soul, at least that was what her father always preached.

She leaned her shoulder against the oak banister and looked over at her mother. "We're not engaged, Mom," she finally said. "We never were."

Her mother frowned in confusion. "I don't understand."

No, she didn't think her mother would. Marilyn Cassidy had never uttered a dishonest word in her life, and she expected her daughters to follow in her footsteps. "I never meant for it to happen," Jill explained, "but after what happened to you and Mrs. Kramer...I didn't want to be the cause of another friendship being destroyed."

Her mother listened quietly while Jill confessed everything, from the date her grandmother had arranged with Luther, to the family's assumption that she'd been engaged, and how it'd just been easier to let everyone assume there had been an important man in her life. She told her mother how she and Morgan met, and even told her the crazy way her insides had fluttered when he'd first looked at her.

She finished by explaining their arrangement and included a few glimpses of Morgan's past so she'd understand why he'd left her when she told him of the promotion she'd been offered.

"You never expected to fall in love with him, did you?" her mother asked after a moment, surprising Jill. She expected at least a few recriminations, but was grateful her mother understood her motives behind the deception. It still didn't lessen her guilt.

The hesitant beginning of a grin tugged Jill's lips. "It was like a freight train, Mom. We were barreling down this track and it was like the brake snapped. Then all of a sudden..."

"You derailed?"

Jill nodded. "With a loud crash," she added.

"Morgan is a good man, Jill. He has responsibilities he takes very seriously. Isn't that part of why you fell in love with him?"

When she didn't answer, her mother asked, "Did you really expect him to give up everything he knows and everything he's worked to build from nothing to follow you to San Francisco?"

Jill twisted the tissue around her fingers. "No, I don't think so. I think I just wanted him to say we could find a way to work it out."

Her mother smoothed her hand comfortingly over Jill's back. "Jilly, how do you expect to work it out if you're not willing to bend a little?"

Jill straightened and looked squarely at her mother. "Me? Why should *I* be the one to bend? You always said that relationships are a compromise. Not always fifty-fifty, sometimes it's seventy-five-twenty-five, sometimes sixty-forty, but in the end they all add up to a hundred. Morgan wasn't even willing to look for a compromise."

Her mother frowned. "And neither were you," she said sternly.

"I almost lost myself once, Mom. I can't do it again. I *won't* do it again."

"But you can expect him to walk away from everything he's ever worked for to follow you to San Francisco. You're asking him to stop being the man you fell in love with. Why? To prove something to you?"

She gave her mother a level stare. "You think I should turn down the promotion, don't you?" she shot out in an accusatory tone. "Just because you walked away from your career doesn't mean I have to."

Her mother's brows knit together in confusion. "Good grief, Jilly. Who planted that silly idea in your head?"

"You. You left med school, Mom. You threw away a career as an M.D. to follow Dad back to Homer and be a preacher's wife. I'm not like you. I'm not like Brenda or Wendy or Ali or Lisa. I won't stop being who I am just to make some man happy." Even if she was head-over-heels in love with him. Even if he did turn her world upside down with a sultry look, a gentle touch or lovemaking more erotic and exciting than she'd ever known existed. She loved Morgan, but she couldn't change who she was...any more than he could.

Jill frowned and looked away. That's exactly what she was asking him to do. Morgan wouldn't ask her to choose him over her promotion, but she'd had no trouble demanding that he walk away from the life he'd built from nothing, a life for himself and the people he cared about. Morgan was a caretaker, and her mother was absolutely right. If he gave up everything he knew for her, he'd no longer be the same man she'd fallen in love with.

"Medicine wasn't *my* dream," her mother said. "That was your grandfather's dream."

Jill shook her head and looked back at her mother. "I remember hearing you say a long time ago that you and Dad almost didn't get married because of your career."

Her mother's smile was as gentle as her blue eyes. "That's true, but not because your father didn't want me to be a doctor. We almost didn't get married because I chose to walk away. He was afraid I'd regret my decision and then resent him. It took a lot of convincing on my part to make him believe that medicine wasn't what I wanted."

"That's where we're different, Mom," Jill said. "I love being a lawyer. It's what I always wanted, what I've worked so hard for all these years. I almost let one man take it away from me. I can't let another."

"Sometimes, Jillian Cassidy, you can be just too stubborn for your own good." Exasperation filled her mother's voice. "Did Morgan ask you to quit being an attorney?"

Jill frowned. "No."

"Did he tell you not to take the job in San Francisco?"

Her frown deepened. "No."

"Then what is he asking of you?"

Jill thought for a moment. "He didn't ask for anything, but if I take that promotion, then our relationship is over. That sure sounds like an ultimatum to me."

"And what happens if you pass on this promotion? Does your job with the firm depend on it?"

"No, but—"

Marilyn let out a long breath and stood. "When you decide what's most important to you, Jilly, then you'll know what you have to do."

"How will I know? What if I make the wrong decision again?"

"Morgan isn't Owen. Owen couldn't love you for who you were, only who he wanted you to be. When you showed him you weren't that person, he tried to change you. Your father and I were so relieved when you called off the wedding."

That couldn't be right. When she'd told her parents she'd called off the wedding, her father had been upset. "But Dad seemed so disappointed."

"In himself, yes. He thought he failed you. All he's ever wanted to do is protect you girls."

"How did he fail me?"

"He so wanted to stop you from marrying Owen, but he knew if he tried, you'd end up getting married just because he said you shouldn't."

As much as it hurt her to admit the truth, her mother was absolutely right. She'd always fought hard to be independent, and if her father had tried to stop her from marrying Owen, she no doubt would have done it just to spite him and to show him she was capable of making her own decisions. "I didn't know."

"For the record," Marilyn added, "Felicia Kramer and I don't speak because I refused to intervene. She wanted your father and I to convince you to marry her son, and we wouldn't do that."

"And now, Mom?" Jill asked, hating the defeated note in her voice. "Can you intervene this time and tell me what to do?"

Marilyn smoothed her hand over Jill's hair. "It has to be your decision. Listen to your heart, sweetie. Your heart will tell you what to do and you'll know."

Jill let out a long breath. "It shouldn't be this hard," she said, and stood.

"It's the tough decisions that define our character," Marilyn answered.

A reluctant grin tugged Jill's lips. "Now you sound like Dad," she said, and hugged her mother. "Thank you, Mom. For listening."

"Why don't you throw some cold water on your face and then come help us in the kitchen. It might just make you feel a little better."

Jill nodded, then climbed the stairs to the bathroom. She knew what she had to do. Turning down that promotion would be difficult, but wrestling with the decision made little sense. She knew what she wanted: Morgan.

The door to her parents' room stood open, and she

slipped inside. She crossed the room to her mother's rolltop desk and sat in the chair, then reached for the telephone. She dialed Nick's number and left a message on his voice mail, asking him to call her, hoping that her mother was right.

And that her heart wasn't lying to her.

MORGAN ORDERED another beer and settled back into the vinyl booth of the Margaritaville Lounge. He had three hours to kill until his flight departed for the coast. Three hours of staring at hot pink and bright turquoise neon flamingos, plastic palms, listening to Jimmy Buffet tunes playing on the jukebox, and thinking about Jill.

The scene had hangover written all over it.

The beer did nothing to mend his heart or numb his mind. Hops and barley were paltry ammunition against the blue-eyed angel who'd stolen his heart when he wasn't looking.

He nursed his beer, cursing himself for being a fool, cursing her for being so damned independent, and cursing her job for taking her away from him. Walking out had been the hardest thing he'd ever done.

"Better now than later," he muttered, then took several more swigs of beer before signaling the waitress for another.

Just like Eleanor, he thought angrily, shoving a twenty toward the edge of the rattan table.

Best to end it now instead of attempting to make a doomed relationship work. First the promotion to senior associate and a relocation. Even if he could follow her to San Francisco, even if he did marry her, her upward mobility wouldn't stop there.

He could see it now. Putting off a family until she made junior partner. Then she'd have to prove herself all over again, put in longer hours, take on more responsibility and postpone children for one more year.

One more year would turn into two or three, and she'd be close to making full partner. She couldn't possibly cut back on her hours to raise a family then.

Finally, six or seven years later would come the promotion to full partner, and even longer hours and more responsibility. By then, when they should be preparing to deal with teenagers and raging hormones, it'd be almost too late to start thinking about babies.

He'd been stupid to think he could change the rules. Rules were established for a reason. Who was he to think he could bend them, even if they were his?

He'd tried and where had it gotten him? On an expressway to a hangover to hide from his breaking heart.

Even if they did attempt to make a go of their relationship, he knew exactly where they'd end up—on opposite sides of a mahogany conference table, and the only ones benefiting would be their respective divorce attorneys.

Hadn't he heard enough from half of his employees on those few occasions he'd joined the men in the shop for a cold one after a long hard day? How many times had he had to find someone else to cover for weekend overtime because Steve, Rick or John had weekend visitation with their kids? The last thing he'd ever want would be weekend father status, or even to become a part-time husband like his old man.

Morgan knew what he wanted: a full-time wife,

and no matter how much he wanted Jill to fill the position, he couldn't accept less.

He'd lived through the ugliness once. He'd seen his parents' marriage crumble with each step Eleanor took toward her own happiness.

Jill's not Eleanor.

Now there was a bit of logic he couldn't argue. Jill was nothing like his mother. Jill was kind and sweet, and she genuinely cared about the people around her. Eleanor cared about no one but herself and her needs.

He let out a sigh and took another long pull on the beer. To be fair, he couldn't honestly claim Eleanor had always been selfish. There were happy times in his childhood. There were family outings and evenings at home with both of his parents filled with love and laughter.

They'd come to a screeching halt the day his mother picked up a briefcase.

Or had they?

He finished off his third beer and briefly considered ordering another, but he was already starting to feel a light buzz and decided to settle for an order of coconut shrimp and black coffee, instead.

He waited for his order and sipped the strong black coffee, hoping to clear his mind in an attempt to resurrect the past. When Eleanor had first gone to work, his old man hadn't been happy, but it had been necessary because of the budget cuts at the university. After a couple of years, Kenneth's class schedule increased again, but Eleanor had refused to give up her position with the advertising agency, fueling the bitterness between his parents.

You belong at home, with your children.

Why can't I have both, Kenneth?

You should have all you want right here at home. Aren't the children and I enough to make you happy?

Morgan signaled for a refill on his coffee. There were more arguments, each more hurtful than the last.

Why can't you be proud of me?

The tearful words slammed into Morgan's memory. His mother crying, more hateful words from his father. Not just during the arguments, but in almost any conversation. If his mother spoke to her children, his father usually had a snide comment to make, until finally Eleanor withdrew completely, not only from her husband, but from her children, as well.

The realization hit him hard. He'd never completely blamed her, and now he understood why. The truth had been buried in his mind. Buried, but not completely forgotten. His father's insecurities had driven Eleanor away to the point she'd eventually shut down emotionally, even from her children.

Just as his own insecurities had him walking out on the woman he loved. It was easier to escape.

The truth sickened him.

He rubbed at the tension building in the back of his neck. How could he have been so blind? How could he have been so stupid as to make the same mistakes his father had? Kenneth and Eleanor had loved once. He was old enough to remember.

Even if his father had been more supportive, his mother's promotion and subsequent transfer to California would still have occurred. The final straw had come when she'd accepted the job without discussing it with his father.

Just like Jill.

Just like her promotion was taking her away from him.

No, Jill hadn't left him; he'd walked out on her. He was no better than his old man. His mother's career hadn't taken her away from her children; his father had pushed her away. He'd systematically belittled and degraded her accomplishments until she'd closed off her emotions and had nothing left to give.

No, the bitterness and resentment had belonged to his father. His mother had her faults, but at least he understood them better now. It didn't change the fact that she'd been cold and unemotional, but those more tender emotions had been stripped away. As he'd told Jill, his mother provided rather than nurtured. What he didn't explain was that Eleanor had forgotten how.

Were his self-imposed rules so important to him because he feared he'd be just like his old man?

But he wasn't his father.

And what about the failed marriage of his friends or his crew? His assistant, Sylvia, was about the only person he knew who had been happily married longer than ten years. In fact, her kids were throwing her and Vince a twenty-fifth anniversary party next month.

So he knew one person who was happily married. It didn't change the fact that Jill would be moving to San Francisco. People depended on him and he couldn't let them down. That didn't mean he didn't support her decision, just that he couldn't see a way for them to be together. Long-distance relationships rarely lasted, and he couldn't settle for anything less than forever.

So what was he going to do about it?

He had no easy solution, but unless he was willing to find one, the woman who touched his soul and captured his heart would be lost to him forever.

And forever was a very long time.

14

JILL STOOD on the brick steps of her father's church, lifting her face to the warmth of the afternoon sunshine. A gentle breeze blowing down from Lake Michigan teased the ends of her hair and ruffled her bangs. The only thing that could have made this day any more perfect would be Morgan by her side. She'd always loved the first day of summer, and in her opinion, Carly couldn't have ordered a more perfect day for her wedding.

She'd spoken to Nick that morning, telling him she couldn't take the promotion if it meant relocating to San Francisco. When he'd asked why, she told him the truth. Her life was with Morgan, and a move up the coast was impossible for him. Thankfully, Nick had been understanding and supportive, even if a little surprised.

Now all she had to do was hope Morgan was equally understanding.

She'd called, but his brother told her he hadn't seen him, which she suspected meant he hadn't been able to get a flight from Chicago to California until this morning. She hadn't bothered to leave a message with Will. She'd be seeing Morgan first thing Monday afternoon when she touched down in L.A. Whether he liked it or not, she wasn't about to let him get away without pleading her case.

She was a lawyer for a reason—when it came to arguments, she knew how to play tough and win.

She turned to go inside. The wedding was being officiated by the minister of a neighboring town, and most of the guests had already arrived and were waiting for the ceremony to begin. Her sisters and mother were waiting in the vestibule for Carly before being seated by the ushers, as had been their tradition since Brenda's wedding to Paul close to ten years ago. Tomorrow morning, following Sunday services, the immediate family would gather at her parents' house for a post-wedding brunch while the bride and groom opened their gifts before heading off to the Florida Keys for their honeymoon.

All eyes turned to her when she stepped into the vestibule. Something was wrong. Her mother's expression was tight and drawn. Worry lined her father's face. Her sisters and Carly's attendants didn't look any less concerned.

"What's going on?" she whispered to Ali.

"Carly's missing."

"Are you sure?"

"Dad just went to get her and she wasn't in the dressing room," Lisa said, smoothing the pink ruffles of baby Francesca's dress.

"She wanted a few minutes alone," Marilyn told her husband. "I just don't understand where she could've disappeared to. She was only alone for ten minutes."

"I'll check the parking lot," Brenda offered, then headed outside.

"Come on, Chickie," Ali said. "Let's go see if she's in Dad's office. Jill, you go see if she's back in the dressing room. Maybe she just went out for a little air."

"I'll go check the house," Wendy offered, then followed Brenda outside.

Jill had her doubts, considering her sister's behavior the past couple of days, but took off toward the dressing room anyway. She pushed through the open door and stepped into the deserted room.

The room was neat and orderly. Carly's makeup bag was gone, as was the bag with the jeans and T-shirt she'd worn to the church that morning. She crossed the plush mint carpeting to the small adjoining bathroom and peered inside. No bride hiding there.

She shouldn't be surprised, yet a small part of her couldn't help but be just a tiny bit shocked that her sister would actually run off without a word to anyone. Carly had always been the good girl, leaving most of the troublemaking to her and Ali.

She closed the bathroom door and turned. Her heart skidded to a halt and her breath stilled for several seconds until joy swept through her.

Morgan.

He looked gorgeous and rumpled. Tiny lines bracketed his eyes, and he looked as if he hadn't slept very well, if at all. The navy slacks he'd worn the night before were wrinkled, and the white dress shirt cuffed at the sleeves wasn't in any better shape. He stepped into the dressing room, closing the door quietly behind him. "Your mother said I'd find you here."

She wanted to charge across the room into his arms. Instead, she exercised caution by folding her hands behind her back and leaning against the doorjamb. "Just looking for the nonexistent bride. You look like hell, by the way. Rough night?"

A grin twitched his lips. "You could say that," he admitted.

She could say a lot of things, like how much she loved him, for starters.

He walked slowly toward her. "I owe you an apology," he said, his low and deep voice rumbling along her nerve endings. "I shouldn't have left like that last night."

She pushed off the doorjamb and met him the last few steps. "Is that why you drove all the way back to Homer?" she asked, searching his face for the truth. "Just to apologize?"

He reached out and cupped her cheek in his warm, callused palm. "That's one of the reasons. I expect groveling and begging forgiveness would be another."

"It's a nice start." She closed her eyes and breathed in his scent, turning toward the warmth. "And the other?"

His thumb lightly brushed her lower lip. "To tell you how much I love you."

Nothing could have kept her out of his arms after that confession. She wreathed her arms around his neck and plastered her body against the hard length of his. He held her tight, as if he was afraid she'd leave if he loosened his hold.

Boy, did he have that wrong!

He caught her lips in a sizzling kiss, deep and thorough and so full of emotion she ached. Her head spun and her mind whirled; her body came alive with instant heat.

"I love you, Jill," he rasped when he ended the kiss. He cupped her face in his hands and looked down at her, the emotion in his thundercloud gaze making her melt all over again.

"I want us to be together," he said. "I haven't worked out the details, and I know it won't be easy at first, but dammit, we have to make it work. I don't want to be without you."

Tears sprang to her eyes. She knew what it cost him to make that promise. "I'm not moving to San Francisco."

His hands fell to his sides and he took a step back. A deep frown fell into place. "You have to. It's your job. You worked for this. You've earned it. You deserve a chance to be happy."

She shook her head and smiled. "I wouldn't be happy in San Francisco. Not if you can't be with me."

"Haven't you been listening? I'm telling you we'll find a way. It might take a while, but I can see about opening another office up north in about a year or so."

She narrowed the distance between them. "You don't have to do that, Morgan. I turned down the promotion."

He shoved a hand through his already disheveled black hair. "Jill, you can't—"

"There'll be other promotions," she interrupted before he took off on another tirade. "And they'll have to be on my terms. I'm not willing to barter our happiness for a few stock options and an office with a window."

"You feel that way now, but what about five years from now? I won't ask you to give that up, Jill."

She smoothed her hand over his chest, smiling when the muscle bunched and jumped where she touched. "You're not asking me to. I won't be giving anything up. I won't lie to you. The law is very important to me, but it doesn't mean a thing if I can't share my life with you. I love *you*, Morgan."

The intensity of his gaze shifted, revealing softer, more tender emotions. Revealing forever.

The door to the dressing room opened. "Any luck?" Brenda asked, then stopped when she spotted the two of them. "Hey, Morgan. Glad to see you came to your senses."

Morgan wouldn't have blamed Jill if she'd told him to get lost, and considering what an insensitive, unsupportive jerk he'd been, part of him was surprised she hadn't told him to hit the highway and don't bother looking back. He'd spent the night in the airport lounge, and two hundred bucks and two rebooked flights later, he'd finally smartened up, caught a couple hours of shut-eye, then headed straight back to Homer, and Jill.

"So am I," he said, never taking his eyes off the one woman who made him re-evaluate his own set of rules.

A flurry of excited voices drifted into the dressing room from the vestibule. "Maybe that's Carly," Jill said. Taking his hand, they left the privacy of the dressing room and followed Brenda to join the rest of her family.

He'd follow her wherever she chose to lead him. His gaze slipped to the gentle sway of her hips beneath the short red dress, then traveled down the length of her gorgeous legs to strappy red high heels that showed off the delicate structure of her feet. He hid a grin. He didn't have to look to know she'd painted her toenails to match.

They stepped into the vestibule. Wendy held out a small white note card. "I found this taped to her mirror. Her car's gone, too."

Jill took the card from Wendy and read it. "I can't do this. Please forgive me. Love, Carly." She looked over at her parents. "She's gone."

"I knew she was nervous," Marilyn said, "but I never expected her to run off like this."

Worry filled the reverend's kind blue eyes. "No one could have predicted Carly would do something so drastic," he told his wife, gently pulling her into his arms.

"Carly will be fine, Dad," Ali said. "Don't worry."

"She's upset and needs her family," Wendy told Ali.

"She needs to be alone," Lisa argued.

Brenda moved to the double doors and peered briefly into the chapel. "What are we going to tell them?" she asked, coming back to join the family.

"Nothing," Morgan said.

He ignored the cries of quiet outrage and turned to Jill. He lifted both of her hands in his and brought them to his lips. "We don't have to tell them anything, other than there's been a change in the program."

She stared up at him with those big blue eyes rounded in surprise and filled with emotion.

"Marry me, Jill."

"Now?"

"Right this second," he said, brushing his lips across her knuckles. "Marry me, Angel, and let me love you for the rest of your life."

Tears filled her eyes, and she laughed and cried at the same time. She tugged her hands free and wrapped her arms around him in a tight embrace.

"I take it this means yes?"

"Yes," she said, nodding, the word muffled against his neck.

A series of soft "aws" and a teary "oh how romantic" came from Jill's older sisters.

He looked over at her parents. Marilyn dabbed her eyes with a lacy handkerchief. "I think it's a beautiful idea," she said, then turned to her husband. "Richard? Don't you agree?"

"Jillian?"

She pulled in a deep breath, then turned in Morgan's arms to face her father.

"Is this what you want?" Reverend Cassidy asked his daughter. "Do you love him?"

She looked up at Morgan and their gazes connected. When he thought of what he'd nearly thrown away...

"Yes, Dad. I love him," she said with such quiet reverence that Morgan's heart swelled.

She really was an angel, he thought, holding her close to his side. An angel who'd effectively cast her spell over him, stealing his heart and his soul.

What he'd thought had been the selling of his soul

had turned into one sweet package of heavenly promise...and the bargain of the century. His angel in red would be his to love for the rest of their lives.

And he was a sucker for a lady in red.

Epilogue

JILL CLOSED HER EYES and moaned in pleasure. "I never imagined my wedding night would be spent quite like this," she said in a breathy whisper.

"Be still," her groom ordered gently. "God knows where this stuff will end up if you don't stop wiggling."

She opened her eyes and looked down at Morgan. "You should have warned me you had a fetish."

"What?" he asked with a rakish grin. "And risk scaring you off before I got to fulfill my fantasy? Not a chance, Angel."

Jill laughed and adjusted the hem of her red chemise. "It'd take more than a desire to paint my toenails to scare me off."

She breathed in the heady scent of roses wafting into their room at the Village Inn through the open French doors, and looked down at her new husband, who was too busy applying another coat of Revlon Red polish to her toenails to notice the silly grin on her face.

As Morgan had predicted, no one had complained too much about the last-minute substitute in the program. Cassidys had flooded into Homer for a wedding, and although the guests had been surprised, at least there'd been a ceremony followed by a reception as originally planned.

There'd been no word from Carly, not that Jill had expected any, other than the brief note she'd left taped to the mirror in her room. She still couldn't quite believe the flash of relief she'd seen on Dean's face when her father had told him of Carly's abrupt departure. Considering Dean's reaction to Carly's prewedding jitters yesterday at the country club, relief had been the last emotion she'd expected from her sister's fiancé.

Her father had always reminded his congregation, as well as his daughters, that things happen for a reason, even if we don't quite understand God's plan. She supposed Carly had a good reason for running away from her own wedding, which only she and the Almighty were privy to, but she couldn't help but be worried about her sister and hoped someone heard from her soon.

"You know," she said, wiggling the toes of her free foot. "We're still living in sin."

"A mere technicality, Mrs. Price," Morgan countered, his deep voice infused with humor. "But we have the good reverend's blessing even if we don't have an actual license. Monday morning we'll make it official with a justice of the peace."

She leaned up on her elbows. "So does this mean we get to have two wedding nights?"

He capped the polish and set the bottle on the nightstand, a wicked grin canting his oh-so-sexy mouth. "I'll give you as many wedding nights as you can handle, Angel. You can count on it."

Now that was something she could definitely get used to. "What about our anniversary? I wonder, does the church wedding count or the legal wedding?"

He eased onto the bed and covered her with his big body, careful not to smudge her freshly painted toenails. "Does it matter?"

She looped her arms around his neck and pressed her lips to his cleanshaven jaw. "Not as long as I get two anniversary nights," she murmured, smoothing her hands over his shoulders and down his torso to tease the towel looped around his waist.

He moved against her and her breath caught. "For a preacher's daughter, you sure do have an insatiable appetite."

She moaned again and tugged the towel from his sculpted body. "Deprivation can do that to a girl," she whispered, lifting her hips to meet his.

Morgan didn't think he'd ever have enough of her, and still couldn't believe his good fortune. He loved her, and for reasons he didn't care to analyze, she returned that emotion, making him realize just how lucky he was.

He slid deep inside her, his heart catching at the desire and heat and love swirling in her hooded blue gaze.

"The last thing I'd want is for my wife to feel deprived," he said, then made her his once again.

Afterward they lay together facing the open French doors as the first rays of pinkish-gray dawn spread across the midwestern sky. Morgan held Jill against him, knowing he'd finally found his own slice of heaven. Marriage, he knew, was a two-way street, sometimes fraught with minor skirmishes, but so long as the base was strong, he and Jill could overcome any obstacles that may be thrown into their path along the way. He was determined not to make the same mistake as his parents, and now understood that compromising required give and take by *both* parties.

"Morgan?"

"Hmm?"

"Have you given any thought to where we're going to live?"

"Does it matter?"

"Well, I was thinking—"

"Uh-oh."

She turned in his arms and gave him a look that said she wasn't amused. He kissed her anyway.

"What if I see about transferring to the San Diego office?" she asked when he finally ended the deep, tongue-tangling kiss. "It's only ninety minutes from Riverside, and if we split the difference and bought a place in between, we'd each only have about a forty-five-minute drive to work. Somewhere in one of those Rancho something-or-another towns on the other side of Temecula."

"Most of my jobs are scheduled into next year and located in or around downtown L.A.," he told her. "We'll have to look into it."

Her honey-gold brows tugged into a frown. "Then maybe that's not such a good idea. What about something in Diamond Bar? It'd only be about an hour or so commute to downtown for me, and less for you, unless of course it's raining, then—"

"Jill?"

She looked up at him, her gaze intent. "Do you have a better idea?"

A wicked grin crossed his lips. "I have a much better plan."

"Ooh," she said in that husky voice he'd never tire of hearing. "Something tells me you're not talking real estate."

He rolled her to her back and leaned over her. "Angel, we'll live wherever you want, so long as we're together."

"I think we should start looking for a four-bedroom house. What do you think?"

"I think we only need one bedroom," he teased, looking down at her.

She shook her head and the teasing light left her eyes. "We'll need four, Morgan. One for us, and one each for Will and Raina when they come home from college."

"And the fourth?"

Her eyes softened and a slow smile spread across her face. "For our son or daughter," she whispered.

Morgan's heart squeezed at the love shining in his wife's eyes, and he knew he'd found what he'd been unconsciously looking for all his life. He forgot about old hurts and concentrated on the future with his own slice of heaven in the last place he'd ever thought to look—the arms of a resourceful, blackmailing angel who had captured his heart, his body and his soul when he'd least expected it.

*Next month,
look for the delightful spin-off
to Jill and Morgan's story!*

1

Rule 1: A lady never cries in public.

THE WILDE SIDE was the last place Cooper Wilde expected to find a fairy princess, but damned if one hadn't just walked through the door. A platinum blond fairy princess with a chickie-boom body and big, round turquoise eyes filled with apprehension. That intriguing gaze darted around the smoky bar before landing on him, sending awareness rumbling through him in Richter-scale-worthy shock waves.

She stood a little straighter and headed right for him as the Red Hot Chili Peppers segued into a classic rock standard by the Hollies. There was nothing long and cool about the hot little number dressed in bridal satin and lace, and Coop seriously doubted she'd ever stepped foot in a bar. Hell, he had suspicions about her even being of the legal age.

She lifted her chin and ignored the stares of his few customers, a blue-collar crowd for the most part, their glances ranging from mild curiosity to a few outright leers that leapt straight across the border toward rude. She tightened her grip on a little satin bag clutched in her delicate fingers and stepped up to the long mahogany bar.

Coop crossed his arms and looked down at her, into those big eyes banked with a determination that filled him with dread. He had enough to worry about in what was becoming a vain attempt to keep the bar operational without having to deal with a jilted bride who didn't have the foresight to change clothes before traipsing around Chicago.

"What can I do for you, Princess?"

"Do you have a pay phone?" she asked in a voice loud enough to be heard over the jukebox.

"In the back," he answered with a quick jerk of his head.

"Thank you," she answered primly.

He braced his hands on the bar and leaned forward. "And you're in the wrong place, Princess. St. Mike's is a few blocks south of here." He pushed off the bar and strolled away, hoping she'd take the hint and leave.

"I'm looking for a telephone, not a church," she called after him.

He shrugged and opened the cooler.

"And I want a drink," the princess yelled over the music in a voice filled with steely determination.

That got his attention. "Not without some ID, Princess. I could lose my license for even allowing you in here."

She gave him a smug look and opened her little satin bag. "As you can see," she said handing over her driver's license, "I'm well over the legal drinking age."

He took the ID from her. "Barely," he muttered, counting backward as he examined the small plastic card, alternately comparing the police line-up quality photo to the real thing. The real thing was much more interesting. Too bad he didn't have time for interesting, because Carly Cassidy was sassy and curvy. Throw in willing, and she was just the way he liked them, even if she was only three years above the legal drinking age.

Coming this September from

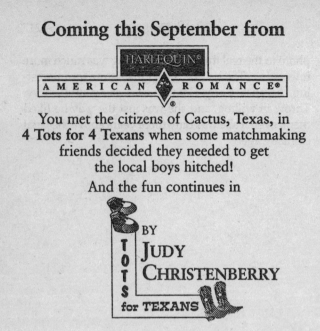

HARLEQUIN®

A M E R I C A N ◆ R O M A N C E®

You met the citizens of Cactus, Texas, in
4 Tots for 4 Texans when some matchmaking
friends decided they needed to get
the local boys hitched!

And the fun continues in

3 TOTS for TEXANS
BY **JUDY CHRISTENBERRY**

Don't miss...

THE $10,000,000 TEXAS WEDDING
September 2000
HAR #842

In order to claim his $10,000,000 inheritance,
Gabe Dawson had to find a groom for Katherine Peters
or else walk her down the aisle himself. But when he
tried to find the perfect man for the job, the list of
candidates narrowed down to one man—*him!*

Available at your favorite retail outlet.

HARLEQUIN®
Makes any time special ™

Visit us at www.eHarlequin.com

HARTOS2

HARLEQUIN

Duets™

Pick up a Harlequin Duets™
from August-October 2000
and receive $1.00 off the
original cover price. *

Experience the "lighter side of love"
in a Harlequin Duets™.
This unbeatable value just became
irresistible with our special introductory
price of $4.99 U.S./$5.99 CAN. for
2 Brand-New, Full-Length
Romantic Comedies.

Offer available for a limited time only.
Offer applicable only to Harlequin Duets™.
*Original cover price is $5.99 U.S./$6.99 CAN.

Visit us at www.eHarlequin.com   HDMKD

If you enjoyed what you just read,
then we've got an offer you can't resist!

Take 2 bestselling love stories FREE!
Plus get a FREE surprise gift!

Clip this page and mail it to Harlequin Reader Service®

IN U.S.A.	IN CANADA
3010 Walden Ave.	P.O. Box 609
P.O. Box 1867	Fort Erie, Ontario
Buffalo, N.Y. 14240-1867	L2A 5X3

YES! Please send me 2 free Harlequin Temptation® novels and my free surprise gift. Then send me 4 brand-new novels every month, which I will receive before they're available in stores. In the U.S.A., bill me at the bargain price of $3.34 plus 25¢ delivery per book and applicable sales tax, if any*. In Canada, bill me at the bargain price of $3.80 plus 25¢ delivery per book and applicable taxes**. That's the complete price and a savings of 10% off the cover prices—what a great deal! I understand that accepting the 2 free books and gift places me under no obligation ever to buy any books. I can always return a shipment and cancel at any time. Even if I never buy another book from Harlequin, the 2 free books and gift are mine to keep forever. So why not take us up on our invitation. You'll be glad you did!

142 HEN C22U
342 HEN C22V

Name	(PLEASE PRINT)	
Address	Apt.#	
City	State/Prov.	Zip/Postal Code

* Terms and prices subject to change without notice. Sales tax applicable in N.Y.
** Canadian residents will be charged applicable provincial taxes and GST.
  All orders subject to approval. Offer limited to one per household.
  ® are registered trademarks of Harlequin Enterprises Limited.

TEMP00   ©1998 Harlequin Enterprises Limited

HARLEQUIN®
Temptation.

Buckhorn County, Kentucky, may not have
any famous natural wonders, but it *does* have
the unbeatable Buckhorn Brothers. Doctor,
sheriff, heartthrob and vet—all different, all
irresistible, all larger than life.

There isn't a woman in town who isn't
in awe of at least one of them.

But somehow, they've managed to hang on
to their bachelor status. Until now...

Lori Foster presents:

Sawyer
#786, On Sale June 2000

Morgan
#790, On Sale July 2000

Gabe
#794, On Sale August 2000

Jordan
#798, On Sale September 2000

The
BUCKHORN
BROTHERS

**All gorgeous,
all sexy, all single.
*What a family!***